$\mathcal{D}$ISNEP

PIRATES of the CARIBBEAN
DEAD MAN'S CHEST

Adapted by Irene Trimble

Based on the screenplay written by
Ted Elliott & Terry Rossio
Based on characters created by Ted Elliott & Terry Rossio
and Stuart Beattie and Jay Wolpert
Based on Walt Disney's Pirates of the Caribbean
Produced by Jerry Bruckheimer
Directed by Gore Verbinski

$\mathcal{D}$ISNEP PRESS
New York

Copyright © 2006 Disney Enterprises, Inc.

All rights reserved. No part of this book may be reproduced or transmitted in any form or by any means, electronic or mechanical, including photocopying, recording, or by any information storage and retrieval system, without written permission from the publisher. For information address Disney Press, 114 Fifth Avenue, New York, New York 10011-5690.
Printed in the United States of America
First Edition
5 7 9 10 8 6
This book is set in Charlotte Book.
Library of Congress Catalog Card Number: 2005905551
ISBN 1-4231-0024-7
Visit www.pirates.movies.com

Chapter 1

The moon rose high above a dark ocean. The quiet sounds of the sea—blowing wind, lapping waves, and creaking lines—filled the night with an eerie symphony. On the walls of a stone prison that overlooked the scene, a flock of crows alighted. The moonlit night was made even eerier by the grunts, moans, and rattling chains of captive prisoners.

A pair of guards dragged a prisoner in through the tower's stone doorway. The passage was clearly the way *into* the prison. The way *out* was very different indeed, as a number of unfortunate captives were about to learn.

More guards, carrying six wooden coffins, made their way to a wall on the prison's seaward side. With a quick condemnation, they shoved each of the coffins off the wall, allowing them to plummet down and splash into the hungry sea below. The coffins bobbed to the surface, and the tide began to carry them out like a fleet of haunted vessels. Two of the pine boxes sailed lower than the rest and began to sink slowly into the black sea.

One of the crows flew down from the prison wall, landing on a coffin. *Peck-peck, peck-peck.* He began to tap away at the wood. *Peck-peck-PECK.* The repetitive *peck-PECK-peck-PECK* was just another sound to fill the shadowy night. *Peck-PECK-peck.* It was also extremely annoying.

The person inside the coffin that the bird had chosen agreed. *Peck-peck-peck-PECK.* Suddenly, a gunshot was fired from inside the coffin that sent the bird blasting off in a cloud of feathers. An arm reached through the newly formed hole, found the latch that held the coffin closed, and swung the lid open. Captain Jack Sparrow, the wiliest pirate ever to sail the high seas, quickly emerged and looked around. He was wearing his usual getup—well-worn clothing, knee-high boots, and his signature red bandanna. His gold tooth gleamed in the moonlight.

Jack didn't seem concerned with his situation . . . at first. Then, his eyes grew wide and he began frantically searching the coffin. After a moment filled with high anxiety, he finally found what he thought he might have lost—his hat! With it placed firmly on his head at a smart angle, Jack was once again relaxed.

He bowed his head, crossed himself, and reached down into the coffin one more time. "Sorry, mate," he said as he pulled and tugged until—SNAP—he plucked off the leg bone of his coffin mate. "Necessity is a mother," he noted with a grin. He used the bone for an oar and rowed toward the moonlit hull of his ship, the *Black Pearl*. She was patiently waiting for him out in the still water, covered by the dark of night.

Gibbs, an old salt and a fine pirate, was waiting on the *Pearl's* deck for Jack's return. "Not quite according to plan?" Gibbs questioned, staring at Jack, who sat rowing a coffin with a leg bone in his hands. Gibbs helped his captain aboard.

"Complications arose," Jack said, tossing the leg bone overboard. "But I've found if you ask right, there's always someone willing to give a leg up."

Gibbs looked over the side of the ship at the one-legged skeleton. "Not in my experience,"

Gibbs said, shaking his head. "Can't go wrong expecting the worst from people."

Jack sighed. "It probably does save time," he said as he walked away from Gibbs. As he moved along the boat, Jack took a rolled piece of cloth from his sleeve. He began to examine it very carefully.

"Is that what you went in to find?" a toothless pirate named Leech asked anxiously. Every man onboard was hungry for news of what treasure Jack had found.

"Aye, but I haven't had time to properly assess the prize," Jack answered with a sly smile. He did not seem willing to share just yet.

Suddenly, a small monkey swung out of the ship's rigging, landed in front of Jack, and screeched as if he were the devil himself. Jack screamed back as the monkey snatched the roll of cloth and took it up into the sails.

Each time the monkey passed through a shaft of moonlight, it turned into a skeleton from head to tail—the result of a curse that had not been lifted. The monkey was the living dead. The horrible little beast's previous owner was the cursed Captain Barbossa, who had mutinied against Jack. Barbossa had named the monkey Jack, as a way to add insult to injury.

Jack hated the creature. He drew his pistol and aimed at the cursed monkey. Jack fired, but the gun only clicked. His shot had already been used on that blasted pecking crow. Jack grabbed a pistol from the belt of another pirate and fired again.

This time he hit his mark. The monkey was blown back, and the cloth dropped from its grasp. But the monkey quickly jumped back up again, grinning.

Gibbs gave Jack a look. "You know that doesn't do any good," he told him, pointing to the gun.

Jack shrugged. "Keeps my aim sharp," he said as one of the pirates on deck scrambled to catch the falling piece of cloth. The monkey continued to screech.

"Why'd that eviscerated simian have to be the only thing to survive *Isla de Muerta*?" Jack grumbled. Then he saw the pirate who had caught the cloth examining it.

"It's a key," the pirate said, cocking his head to the side and squinting an eye.

"Even better," Jack added, raising a finger. "It's a *drawing* of a key."

The confused crew looked to Gibbs for an explanation.

"Captain," Gibbs said, clearing his throat, "I think we were expecting something a bit more . . . rewarding. What with *Isla de Muerta* going all pear shaped, reclaimed by the sea and all . . ."

"Unfortunate turn of circumstance," Jack agreed, remembering the island, where the crew had its most recent adventure, where Jack finally defeated Barbossa, *and* where he had reclaimed the *Black Pearl*.

". . . and then spending months fighting to get the British navy off our stern," Gibbs reminded him.

"Inevitable outcome of *le vie de boucanier*," Jack replied with a wave of his hand.

"We've been losing crew at every port, and it seems to us what's left that it's been a stretch since we've done even a speck of honest pirating," Gibbs continued.

Jack turned to his crew. "Is that how you're feeling?" he asked. "That I'm not serving your interests as captain?"

The crew shifted uncomfortably, and then

suddenly, a parrot squawked the only reply, "ABANDON SHIP!"

The parrot belonged to the mute pirate Cotton, and it spoke for him.

Jack drew his pistol again. "What did the bird say?"

"Cotton's parrot don't speak for the lot of us," Leech told Jack quickly. "*We* think you're doing a fine job."

"ABANDON SHIP," the parrot called out even louder. Jack was about to shoot the old bird, but lowered his gun instead. Cotton seemed relieved.

"At least there's one honest . . . man amongst you," Jack said, looking at Cotton's parrot. Jack shook his head and got down to the business at hand. He had questions to answer.

"Gentlemen, what do keys do?" Jack asked.

The anxious crew of rogues looked at each other. "They unlock things?" Leech asked, suddenly excited.

Jack made a face as if to say, "Yes, and . . ."

"And whatever this unlocks, inside is something valuable," Gibbs added, imagining chests of gold. "So, we're setting out to find whatever this unlocks!"

Jack shook his head. "No. If we don't have the key, we can't open whatever it unlocks, so what purpose would be served in finding whatever needs be unlocked without first having found the key that unlocks it? Honestly. Ninny."

The rowdy crew was very confused. They tried to follow along as best they could. "So, we're going to find this key?" Gibbs asked.

Jack looked into the crew members' blank faces and sighed. "What good is a key if we have nothing for the key to unlock? Please," Jack pleaded, "try and keep up!"

"So, do we have a heading?" another pirate asked.

"Aye! A heading!" Jack said. He turned away, took out his Compass, and flipped it open. It was the very same Compass that had led him to *Isla de Muerta* and the caves of hidden treasure. But the readings on the Compass seemed to make Jack a bit uneasy now.

He snapped the Compass shut and waved his arm. "Set sail in a general . . . that way direction," he finally said, waving his hand dismissively out toward the sea.

"Captain?" Gibbs asked, confused. This was not typical Captain Jack Sparrow behavior.

"I'll plot our course later. Now snap to and make sail!" he ordered as he marched off to his cabin. The crew stood and watched silently. "You know how it works!" Jack shouted impatiently and slammed his cabin door.

The crew unhappily began to get ready to sail. "Have you noticed lately, the captain seems to be acting a bit . . . strange?" a pirate whispered to Gibbs.

"Aye," Gibbs answered. "Something's got him setting a course without knowing his own heading. And I thought there was neither man nor beast alive could make him do that."

Chapter 2

While Jack's crew dealt with their captain's stranger-than-usual behavior, a couple who should be celebrating the happiest day of their lives was trying to avert disaster—a ruined wedding.

Outside a small seaside chapel in the Caribbean town of Port Royal, palm trees bent in the wind as rain drenched all the preparations for the nuptial celebration to be held that day. The bride, Elizabeth Swann, kneeled in her rain-soaked wedding dress, tears mixing with rain. Around her was an empty altar, overturned chairs . . . and no groom. Slowly, the young woman rose and entered the chapel to wait, her head in her hands.

The approaching sound of chains made Elizabeth look up. Through her tears she saw a man in uniform enter the chapel. He was followed by a company of marines who were dragging a prisoner. To her shock, it was her groom, Will Turner.

"Will!" Elizabeth called out. "What is happening?"

Will struggled toward her. "I don't know," he said sadly, taking in Elizabeth's ruined white satin dress.

Will had been taken prisoner earlier when marines battered down the door of his blacksmith shop and put him in irons. It didn't look like he'd be married today, after all. But waiting for his future wife, Elizabeth, was something Will was used to. He had loved her since Elizabeth and her father, the Governor of Port Royal, found Will drifting on the sea when he was ten years old. For years, he had waited patiently, hoping she would finally love him back. And then she had. But it seemed that once again, they would be kept apart.

Even now, standing there in chains, he couldn't help getting sentimental. "You look beautiful," Will said softly.

Elizabeth smiled. "You know it's bad luck for the groom to see the bride before the wedding."

"That explains the unexpected guests," he said, nodding to the company of red-coated marines surrounding them.

Their tender moment was interrupted by an authoritative voice. It was Elizabeth's father.

"You! Order your men to stand down and remove these shackles at once," the governor commanded.

The man in charge of the arrest made no move. "Governor Weatherby Swann," he answered. "My apologies for arriving without an invitation."

Governor Swann studied the man's face for a moment. "Cutler Beckett?" he finally asked.

"It's *Lord*, now, actually," Beckett replied.

"Lord or not, you have no reason and no authority to arrest this man."

"In fact, I do. Mr. Mercer?" he said to an undistinguished-looking gentleman standing off to the side. Mercer opened a large dispatch case and handed Beckett several documents.

Beckett ceremoniously read off his newly appointed powers by the Royal Commission for Antilles Trade and Protection, then produced a warrant for the arrest of one William Turner.

Governor Swann looked at the warrant. But it wasn't for Will. "This is for Elizabeth Swann!" he exclaimed.

"Is it?" Beckett asked. "How odd . . . my mistake. Arrest her," he suddenly ordered.

The soldiers grabbed Elizabeth. "On what charges?" Elizabeth demanded.

Beckett ignored her as he shuffled through his papers. "Aha," he said, holding up another document. "Here's the warrant for William Turner. And I have another one for a James Norrington. Any idea where he is?"

"Commodore Norrington resigned his commission several months ago," Governor Swann answered quickly, "and we haven't seen him since."

Elizabeth gritted her teeth. She had once been betrothed to Norrington, though she never loved him. She suddenly found herself thinking about all she and Will—and Jack Sparrow—had been through.

Elizabeth was kidnapped by Barbossa and his men. To rescue her from the cursed pirate, Will had broken Jack Sparrow out of jail, only to be captured himself. In desperation, Elizabeth had agreed to marry Norrington in exchange for his help in saving Will. When the adventure had ended, Norrington had grudgingly agreed to give Jack Sparrow a day's head start before he would begin chasing him. It was only fair, as the pirate had saved Elizabeth. But even though it was the fair thing to do, Norrington had never forgiven himself for letting Sparrow slip away. He had lost his post and disappeared from Port Royal, disgraced.

"We are British subjects under jurisdiction of the King's Governor of Port Royal, and we demand to know the charges against us," Elizabeth said bravely, coming back to the present.

Beckett looked at his prisoners. When he finally spoke up, he sounded more than happy to make his announcement. "The charge is conspiring to secure the unlawful release of a convict condemned to death. For which, regrettably, the punishment is also death. You do remember a pirate named, I believe it is, Jack Sparrow?"

Will and Elizabeth exchanged a look. "*Captain* Jack Sparrow," they said in unison.

"Yes. I thought you might," Beckett answered, satisfied. He motioned to his men to haul the prisoners away.

Chapter 3

While Will and Elizabeth tried to sort out their current mess, Captain Jack Sparrow was dealing with problems of his own. Alone in his cabin aboard the *Black Pearl*, Jack held his Compass tightly in his hand. He sneaked a look at it once, snapped it shut, shook it, and looked again. *Still* not to his liking, Jack reached for a bottle of rum. As the tattered cuff of his sleeve fell back, the branded letter *P* showed on his wrist.

Jack raised the bottle and sighed. It was empty. "Why is the rum always gone?" he asked himself. He lurched toward the cabin door and onto the main deck in search of another bottle.

"Heading, Captain?" Leech asked as Jack staggered past the wheel.

"Steady as she goes," Jack ordered, stumbling toward the ship's hold.

Below deck, pirates snored loudly as they

slept in their hammocks. A cage of chickens clucked as Jack entered. The captain raised his pistol and the chickens suddenly went quiet.

"That's what I thought," Jack said. Then he continued on.

Steadying himself on the ship's timbers, Jack made his way to the rum locker. He raised an eyebrow as he checked the racks. All were nearly empty.

Happily, Jack spied a bottle on a lower shelf and tugged it free. The bottle was encrusted with barnacles. Something was wrong. Jack uncorked it, looked inside, and turned it over. Sand spilled out onto the deck.

"Time's run out, Jack," a voice suddenly said from the shadows. Jack turned. The face he saw was covered with starfish and barnacles. Crabs crawled up the man's arm as he stepped toward Jack.

"Bootstrap?" Jack asked, barely recognizing the voice. "Bill Turner?"

"Aye, Jack Sparrow. You look good."

Jack looked at the gruesome sailor. He wished he could say the same for him. He actually tried a few times, but couldn't bring himself to say it.

"Is this a dream?" Jack asked instead.

"No," Bootstrap Bill Turner, Will's father, answered flatly.

Jack shrugged. "I thought not. If it were, there'd be rum."

Bootstrap grinned and offered Jack a bottle. Jack pried the bottle from Bill's hand, uncorked it, and sniffed it to be sure. Rum it was. Jack wiped the mouth of the bottle with his sleeve and took a long drink.

Bootstrap watched. "You got the *Pearl* back, I see." But Jack couldn't focus on his old shipmate's words. He was staring at the slithering, sliding sea life that lived on the man's skin.

The captain snapped himself out of it. "I had some help retrieving the *Pearl*. Your son," Jack said.

Bootstrap looked surprised. "William? He ended up a pirate, after all?"

Jack nodded, then added, "He's got an unhealthy streak of honest to him."

"That's something, then," Bill told him. "Though no credit to me." The crustacean-crusted pirate fell silent.

"And to what do I owe the pleasure of your carbuncle?" Jack finally asked.

"Davy Jones," Bootstrap answered. "He sent me as an emissary."

Jack had been expecting this. "Ah, he shang-haied you into service, then."

"I chose it. I'm sorry for the part I played in mutinying against you," Bootstrap said sincerely. Jack waved it off and took another swig of rum. Bootstrap had been part of the *Black Pearl*'s crew when Barbossa mutinied. All the rest of the crew had decided to follow Barbossa and make him their captain. Jack had been left on an island to die.

"Everything went wrong after that," Bootstrap told him. "I ended up cursed, doomed to the depths of the ocean, unable to move, unable to die."

Jack shuddered.

"All I could do was think," Bootstrap continued. "And mostly I thought if I had even the tiniest hope of escaping this fate, I would take it. Trade anything for it."

"That is the kind of thinking bound to catch *his* attention," Jack said, knowing more than a bit about Jones's love for a good bargain.

"It did," Bootstrap said, nodding with regret.

"Davy Jones came. Made the offer. I could spend one hundred years before his mast, with the hope that after, I would go on to a peaceful rest."

Bootstrap stopped talking and looked his former captain in the eye. Then he added, "You made a deal with him, too, Jack. He raised the *Pearl* from the depths for you, and thirteen years you've been her captain."

"Technically . . ." Jack said, about to object, but Bootstrap stopped him.

"You won't be able to talk your way out of this," Bootstrap warned as a crab crawled down his arm. The cursed pirate crushed it and shoved it into his mouth. "The terms what applied to me, apply to you, as well. One soul, bound to crew a lifetime aboard his ship."

But Jack wasn't about to let himself start looking like old Bootstrap anytime soon. "The *Flying Dutchman* already has a captain," Jack argued, pointing out that Jones was the captain of the ghostly ship. "So, there's no need of me."

Bootstrap expected as much from Jack. Captain Jack Sparrow never went down without a fight. Bootstrap sighed and nodded. "Then it's the locker for you, Jack. Jones's leviathan will find you and drag the *Pearl* back to the depths . . . and you along with it."

"Any idea when Jones will release said terrible beastie?" Jack asked, trying not to sound too worried.

Bootstrap raised an arm and pointed to Jack's hand. Jack took a step back, but it was too late. On his palm appeared the dreaded Black Spot. Jack stared at it. He was now a marked man.

"It's not a matter of how long till it comes after you," Bootstrap said as Jack looked down at the spot. "It's a matter of how long till you're found."

Jack looked up and Bootstrap Bill was gone. Jack let out a yelp and ran.

"On deck!" he yelled to his sleeping crew as he passed through the hold. "All hands! Lift the skin up. Scurry! Movement, I want movement!"

As the groggy pirates dragged themselves to their stations, Jack looked into the *Pearl*'s black sails. "Haul those sheets!" he ordered the men. "Haul 'em! Run, mates, run, as if the devil himself is on us!"

While the crew was distracted, Jack wrapped his hand in a rag to cover the Black Spot. He couldn't let anyone see that he was marked.

Gibbs looked for Jack and found him hiding behind the mast.

"Do we have a heading?" he asked.

"Land!" Jack yelled back.

"What port?" Gibbs asked.

"I said land! Any land!" Just then "Jack" the monkey jumped from the rigging, landed on Jack's shoulder, and knocked the captain's hat overboard.

"Jack's hat!" Gibbs cried, knowing how fond of it the captain was. "Bring the ship about!"

"No!" Jack snapped. "Leave it."

Jack's crew stood stunned. They knew how much the hat meant to him. They could not believe he would actually *not* want to retrieve it. "Mind your stations, the lot of you!" Gibbs ordered, and then he turned to Jack. "For the love of mother and child, Jack, what's coming after us?"

Chapter 4

Captain Jack Sparrow's legendary three-cornered hat floated on the tide, turning slowly. By next morning, it had drifted far from the *Black Pearl*.

The hull of a small fishing vessel passed it, and suddenly the hat was snatched up by a boat hook. A short, round sailor pulled it from the water and was pleased with the look of the hat. He quickly tried it on.

Just then, his mate yanked it off his head. The two were pulling on the hat when a shudder suddenly ran through the boat. The men stopped struggling.

From beneath the deck came a loud crunching. The sailors staggered as their little vessel rocked. They looked wildly around and then down at the hat. The strange turn of events must have something to do with the hat! The sailors fought to rid themselves of it.

But the fight ended quickly, as the deck splintered and the entire boat was pulled straight down. A giant geyser rose up from the sea, raining down wood and bits of canvas. And, in the blink of an eye, the water was still and the fishing boat was no more.

Not far away, in the headquarters of the East India Trading Company, Will Turner was escorted by two guards into the office of Lord Beckett. A large, unfinished map of the world took up one whole wall of the office.

"Those won't be necessary," Beckett said, pointing to the shackles on Will's wrists.

The guards released Will. "Do you intend to release Elizabeth, as well?" Will asked.

"That is entirely up to you," Beckett answered, and then quickly rephrased his response. "That is entirely *dependent* on you," he clarified. Beckett used his cane to stoke the room's fireplace. "We wish for you to act as our agent in a business transaction with our mutual friend, Captain Sparrow."

"More acquaintance than friend," Will said. "How do *you* know him?"

"We've had dealings in the past," Beckett said displaying the letter *P* on the end of his glowing cane. The same *P* brand that was burned into Jack's arm. "We have each left our marks on the other."

"What mark did he leave on you?" Will asked, but Beckett did not respond. Instead, he said, "By your efforts, Jack Sparrow was set free. I ask you to go to him and recover a certain property in his possession."

"Recover," Will said skeptically. "At the point of a sword?"

Beckett smiled. "Bargain," he suggested slyly. "To mutual benefit and for fair value."

He removed several large documents from his desk. They were signed by the King of England. "Letters of Marque," Beckett explained. "You will offer what amounts to a full pardon. Jack will be free, a privateer in the employ of England."

Will looked at the letters and shook his head. He knew that the Letters of Marque would give him the right to take Jack's possessions, but something didn't feel right. "For some reason, I doubt Jack will consider employment to be the same as freedom," Will pointed out.

"Jack Sparrow is a dying breed," Beckett snarled. He motioned to the map on the wall. "The world is shrinking, the blank edges of the map filled in. Jack will have to find a place in the New World, or perish.

"Not unlike you," Beckett continued, bringing the point home. "You and your fiancée face the hangman's noose. Certainly, that's motivation enough for you to convince Captain Sparrow to accept our offer. And for you to accept, as well, Mr. Turner."

Will considered the proposal. "So you'll get both Jack and the *Black Pearl*."

Beckett seemed surprised. "The *Black Pearl*? No, Mr. Turner, the item in question is considerably smaller and far more valuable, something Sparrow keeps on his person at all times. A Compass."

Beckett noticed a look of recognition on Will's face.

"Ah, you know it," Beckett hissed. Then he added, "Bring back the Compass or there is no deal!"

Will Turner stormed out of Beckett's office and through the gates of the Port Royal prison. He pushed past the red-coated guard and moved down the stone corridor to Elizabeth's cell. Governor Swann followed closely behind.

"Here, now!" the guard called out. "You can't be here, Mister Swann!"

"*Governor* Swann," he said correcting the guard. "I'm not wearing this wig to keep my head warm, you know." Swann looked into the guard's face. "Carruthers, isn't it? Enjoy your job, Mr. Carruthers?"

The guard quickly changed his tone. "Yes, sir. Particularly when the folks come up to visit the prisoners."

"Very good," Swann said. He nodded toward the door and the guard quickly exited.

As the governor approached the dank cell, he heard Elizabeth say to Will, "Jack's Compass? Why would Beckett want that?"

Elizabeth was behind bars, still in her wedding dress. "Does it matter?" Will asked. "I'm to find Jack and convince him to return to Port Royal. In exchange, the charge against us will be dropped."

Will stepped as close to Elizabeth as possible with bars between them. "If I hadn't set Jack free . . ." he began, trailing off regretfully. "I never expected you would bear the consequences."

Elizabeth smiled. "I share the consequences gladly." She reached through the bars and took his hands. "How are you going to find him?" she asked anxiously.

Her confidence touched Will's heart. He suddenly felt he could do anything. "Tortuga. I'll start there, and not stop searching until I find him, and then I will come back here, and marry you."

"Properly?" Elizabeth asked.

"Eagerly," Will promised.

Chapter 5

Will Turner started his search immediately. He would check every island in the Caribbean if he had to—he was going to find Jack. He made his way to Tortuga, stopping at various island ports on the way. On one, he walked up the dock and asked the first man he saw of Jack's whereabouts.

"Captain Jack Sparrow?" the weathered sailor answered. "Owes me four doubloons. Heard he was dead."

Down a cobblestone alley on another island, Will made his way into a candlelit tavern. The innkeeper, a square, thickset man, told Will, "Ran off with a Creole woman to Madagascar." Then he added with a wink, "She was half his age and twice his height!"

On a beach a half-blind fisherman told his version. "Singapore is what I heard. Sure as the tide," he nodded with a toothless grin, "Jack Sparrow will turn up in Singapore!"

Will sighed. There were a thousand tales about Jack Sparrow's whereabouts. Will had one last chance to get the truth—ironically, in a place where truth was hard to come by—Tortuga!

Tortuga was a well-known haunt of Captain Jack Sparrow's. It was the dirtiest port in all the Caribbean; a place for drunken pirates on the lookout for fresh risks and high adventure. A place, Will remembered as the stench of Tortuga filled his nostrils, Jack held dear to his heart.

As soon as Will arrived, he saw a woman he had met the last time he had been to Tortuga with Jack. The woman had red hair and wore a red dress. Her name, if he remembered correctly, was Scarlett. He figured he'd ask her if she'd seen Jack recently.

"I haven't seen him in a month," Scarlett snapped. "When you find him, give him a message." She raised her hand and struck Will across the face before stalking off.

Rubbing his cheek as he walked on, Will noticed a shrimper on the deck of a small boat.

"Can't say 'bout Jack Sparrow," the shrimper told Will as he pulled in his nets. "But there's an island just south of the straits where I trade spice for *mmmmm* delicious long pork. No, can't say for Jack, but you'll find a ship there, a ship with black sails."

For a few coins, Will convinced the shrimper to sail him out to the island. As they came around the point, Will saw it for himself; the *Black Pearl* careened onto the sand! His spirits soared.

"My brother, he will row you to shore," the shrimper told Will. He gave a taller, round-faced man a nod as Will climbed into his tiny rowboat. But halfway to the beach, the brother told Will, "No," and began to turn the boat around.

"What's wrong?" Will asked. "The beach is right there." But the man only rowed faster back toward the shrimp boat.

Will had no choice. He shook his head, dove in, and swam to the shore.

Soaking wet, Will walked over the beach toward the *Black Pearl*. The huge ship rested, wedged into the sand. No noise came from her decks.

A bit further on, Will found the remains of a campfire. He felt the ashes. They were still warm. Jack must have been here. He had to be close!

"Jack!" Will called out. "Jack Sparrow! Mister Gibbs! Anyone . . ."

Will turned toward the dense jungle and saw a flutter in the branches. It was Cotton's parrot!

"Good to see a familiar face," Will said to the old bird, now even surer Jack and the crew were on the island.

"Don't eat me!" the parrot squawked.

"I'm not even hungry," Will said as he looked for a path through the jungle.

"DON'T EAT ME!" the parrot screamed even louder.

Will turned his attention back to the bird. "Look, you're nothing but feathers and bones and you probably taste like pigeon." The parrot went silent.

"Sorry," Will said, feeling badly. "That was uncalled for. Listen . . . if anyone should ask, tell them Will Turner went into the jungle in search of Jack Sparrow. Understand?" Will sighed. "I'm talking to a parrot," he said to himself.

"Aye, aye, sir!" the parrot answered, bobbing his head.

Will grinned, drew his sword, and began hacking into the jungle. He cut through the huge leaf of a palm and noticed a small, red flask on the jungle floor. "Gibbs . . ." Will said quietly, recognizing the old pirate's flask.

He crouched down to pick it up and noticed a trip wire was attached. Will smiled, thinking the pirates had set a trap. Holding on to the wire he followed it to a tree. Suddenly, two eyes appeared in the tree trunk as a perfectly camouflaged arm reached out and yanked the trip wire hard.

In an instant, Will was pulled off his feet and dangled upside down. As he hung by his leg, he suddenly saw a group of the island's warriors. They had bite marks all over their faces and bodies, and were wearing what looked like human bones! No wonder the shrimper had been so frightened. The warriors lunged at him with their spears raised. Will kicked off the tree and knocked several of them to the ground.

"Come on!" Will said, provoking a bit-up warrior. "I'm right here!"

The warrior raised a blowgun and fired a dart into Will's neck. Will went limp, and the warrior cut him down.

Chapter 6

Meanwhile, in a dank cell in Port Royal, Elizabeth could do nothing but wait. Moonlight poured through the cell's small window and cast shadows on the wall. She was exhausted and had just closed her eyes when she heard the jangle of keys.

"Come quickly!" she heard a voice that sounded like her father's call out.

Governor Swann stepped out from the shadows. "What's happening?" Elizabeth asked. The guard swung open the door, and Elizabeth hurried out of her cell. Governor Swann gave the guard a nod.

"I've arranged passage for you back to England," Governor Swann said as he and his daughter ran quickly down a torchlit corridor. "The captain is an old friend."

The governor led Elizabeth to a waiting

carriage, but Elizabeth refused to get in. She was waiting for Will.

"We cannot count on Will's help," the governor said desperately, drawing a pistol. "Beckett has offered only one pardon. One. And it has been promised to Sparrow. Do not ask me to endure the sight of my daughter walking to the gallows! Do not!" He pushed her inside and pressed the pistol into her hand. Then he shut the door and hastily drove the carriage to the waiting ship.

As they neared the dock, the governor slowed his horses to a stop. Two men stood huddled in the shadows. One of them wore a captain's hat.

"Stay inside," the governor said to Elizabeth as he leapt down. He hurried over to the two men. "Captain Hawkins!" the governor said, relieved to see a friend.

But Hawkins did not answer. The other man stepped away and the captain slumped forward, his tunic covered in blood. Governor Swann suddenly realized the other man in the shadows had been holding the captain's body upright.

"Evening, Governor," the man said, slowly wiping the blood from his knife with a handkerchief. Swann gasped. He recognized the man. It was Mercer, Beckett's clerk.

"Shame, that," Mercer said as he motioned toward the body. Governor Swann bolted toward the carriage in a panic. "Elizabeth!" he cried out. But with a whistle, Mercer had a company of troops assembled.

Mercer smiled and yanked the carriage door open himself. It was empty.

"Where is she?" Mercer demanded angrily.

"Who?" Swann asked.

Mercer slammed the governor against the carriage and snarled, "Elizabeth!"

"She was always a willful child," the governor offered innocently. Mercer ordered the man put in irons and, with a violent jerk, led him away.

Chapter 7

Lord Beckett entered his dark office inside the East India Trading Company building. He lit a lamp on his large mahogany desk and noticed that the case that held the Letters of Marque was empty. He also sensed he was not alone.

Elizabeth stepped from the shadows and raised the pistol her father had given her. "These Letters of Marque," Elizabeth said, slapping the documents to his desk. "They are signed by the king, but blank."

Beckett smiled, unafraid. "And not valid until they bear my signature and seal."

"I have information," Elizabeth said, the gun steady in her hand. "You sent Will to get you the Compass owned by Jack Sparrow," she continued. "It will do you no good. I have been to *Isla de Muerta*. I have seen the treasure myself. There is something you need to know."

Beckett smiled smugly. "Ah, I see. You think the Compass points only to *Isla de Muerta*. I am afraid you are mistaken, Miss Swann. I care not for cursed Aztec Gold," Beckett said, recalling the treasure trove in the cave where Jack defeated Barbossa. "My desires are not so provincial."

Lord Beckett motioned to a huge world map. "There is more than one chest of value in these waters," he said. "So perhaps you wish to enhance your offer. . . ." he finished with a smile.

Elizabeth drew the hammer back on the pistol and leveled it at Lord Beckett's head. He suddenly stopped laughing.

"Consider into your calculations that you robbed me of my wedding night," Elizabeth said sternly.

At gunpoint, Beckett signed the papers, but he did not immediately hand them over.

"You are making great effort to ensure Sparrow's freedom," Beckett said, curious.

"These are not going to Jack," Elizabeth replied.

"Then to ensure Mr. Turner's freedom. And what about me? I'll still want the Compass. Consider that in your calculations."

With that, Beckett released his hold on the Letters of Marque. Elizabeth now had what she had come for. She turned and disappeared into the dark.

The following morning, a merchant vessel, the *Edinburgh Trader*, sailed from Port Royal. As the ship moved into open water, a sailor on deck came upon something strange. He picked it up; it was a wedding dress.

Captain Bellamy heard the commotion and immediately came on deck. His bursar and quartermaster were trying to pull the dress from each other's grip.

"If both of you fancy the dress," Captain Bellamy shouted, "you'll just have to share, and wear it one after the other."

"It's not like that, sir," the bursar answered swiftly. "The ship is haunted!"

Bellamy looked at the dress. "Is it, now?"

"Aye," the quartermaster agreed. "There's a female presence here with us, sir . . . everyone feels it."

The crew began to grumble. "Ghost of a lady widowed before her marriage, I figure it," a sailor said and spat neatly, "searching for her husband lost at sea."

The bursar nodded. "We need to throw it overboard, and hope the spirit follows, or this ship will taste the icy waters in a fortnight, mark my words!"

A sailor painting the rail listened closely to the argument.

"Enough!" Captain Bellamy ordered. He took the dress and examined it closely. "Men, this appears to me nothing more as we have a stowaway onboard. A young woman, by the looks of it. To your duties. And if there is a stowaway and 'tis a woman, I don't see she's likely to escape without notice, aye?"

The crew considered this for a moment, and then scattered, all searching for the lady. The sailor who was painting the rail turned to face the rest of the crew.

But it wasn't a sailor at all. It was Elizabeth, well disguised in sailor's clothes. She put down her paintbrush and joined the search for the lady onboard, all but unnoticed by the rowdy gang.

Chapter 8

Meanwhile, in a distant jungle, Will Turner awoke to find himself tied up and being paraded through a small village filled with huts. The island's inhabitants watched the procession with curiosity. Finally, Will was set down before a huge throne.

He looked up . . . and smiled. Sitting on the throne, dressed in ornate ceremonial garb, was none other than Captain Jack Sparrow!

"Jack Sparrow," Will said. "I can honestly say I am glad to see you."

Jack didn't respond. He just stared blankly at Will. It was as though he had never seen Will before.

The warriors pushed Will forward. "Jack? Jack, it's me, Will Turner. Tell them to let me go."

Jack stepped down from his throne and gave Will's arm a pinch. He spoke in a language Will had never heard. The warriors nodded. Will suddenly noticed the throne was no ordinary throne—it was made of human bones.

"Jack, listen," Will said desperately. "The Compass. That's all I need. Jack, Elizabeth is in danger. We were arrested for helping *you*. She faces the gallows!"

Motioning toward Will's leg, one of the warriors hungrily rubbed his belly, suggesting that Will would make a fine meal. Jack nodded and the tribe cheered.

"No!" Will shouted as the warriors grabbed him. "Jack, what did you tell them?" But Jack didn't answer. He climbed back on his throne and stared off into the distance.

As the warriors dragged Will past Jack to prepare him for dinner, Jack's eyes rolled wildly in his head, catching Will's attention. "Save me!" Jack whispered desperately out of the corner of his mouth.

The warriors dragged Will to a chasm where two cages made from bones hung from thick rope. Will noticed that some of the crew of the *Black Pearl* were trapped in the cages. Before Will could react, he was tossed into a cage.

"Ah, Will, you shouldn't have come!" Gibbs shouted in greeting.

Will struggled to his feet, then reached into his pocket. He handed Gibbs the flask he had found on the jungle floor. Gibbs raised it as Will asked about Jack's odd behavior and leader status over the tribe.

"Why would he do this to you?" Will asked, looking around at the caged crew. "If Jack is the chief . . ."

"Aye," Gibbs answered dismally, "the Pelegostos made Jack their chief, but he stays chief for only so long as he *acts* like a chief . . . which means he cannot do anything they think a chief ought not do."

"He's a captive, then," Will said, "as much as any of us."

Gibbs frowned. "Worse, as it turns out. The Pelegostos believe that Jack is a god, trapped in human form. They intend to do Jack the honor of releasing him from his fleshy prison."

Out of the corner of his eye, Will noticed Cotton add his two cents. He mimed something about being cut up with a knife. Will frowned.

"They'll roast and eat him. It's a deeply

held religious belief," Gibbs mused. "Or, we figure, maybe they just get awful hungry."

Will could see most of the crew between the two cages, but a good many pirates were gone. "Where's the rest of the crew?" he asked.

"These cages we're in," Gibbs sighed, "wasn't built till after we got here."

Will looked at the cages of human bone and quickly removed his hand.

"The feast starts when the sun sets," Gibbs said gravely. "Jack's life will end . . . when the drums stop."

Chapter 9

In a small boat, just offshore, two pirates in worn clothing, Pintel and Ragetti, rowed with their backs to the setting sun. The bumbling duo was all that remained of Barbossa's crew. Ragetti, the tall thin one, held a book in his lap. ". . . and I say it was divine providence what escaped us from jail," he said, adjusting his wooden eye.

"And I say it was me being clever," Pintel, the shorter one, replied and kept rowing. A dog with a ring of keys in its mouth suddenly raised its head at the bow. Pintel patted the dog on the head. "Ain't that right, poochie?"

"How do you know it wasn't Divine Providence what inspired you to be clever?" Ragetti argued. "Anyways, I ain't stealing no ship."

"It ain't stealing," Pintel said as they neared the point of the small island, "it's salvaging, and since when did you care?"

"Now that we're not immortal no more," Ragetti said nervously, "we need to take care of our immortal souls." He looked down at the book in his lap.

"You know you can't read!" Pintel shouted at him.

"It's the Bible," the wooden-eyed pirate Ragetti said, smiling, his teeth broken and brown, "you get credit for trying."

"Pretending to read the Bible is a lie, and that's a mark against ya," Pintel yelled when the *Black Pearl* suddenly came into view. They'd been looking for it for what seemed like forever, and now . . .

"Look! There it is!" Pintel cried.

The dog suddenly jumped into the clear blue water and swam for shore. "What's got into him?" Pintel asked.

"Must have spotted a *cat*fish," Ragetti chuckled.

As they reached the shore, Pintel looked up at the ship's black sails. "It's ours for the taking!" he said greedily, as the sound of drums began to suddenly sound through the jungle and out to the sandy beach.

Chapter 10

The beat of the drums was building as the Pelegostos prepared for their grand feast. As they gathered wood for the fire pit, their guest of honor, and main course, Captain Jack Sparrow nodded his approval and tried to force a smile. "I notice women here, but very few children . . . why is that? Are the little ones most tasty?" he asked.

Jack didn't get an answer. The warriors were busy placing a large spit over the fire pit. Jack gulped and took a breath. "Not big enough!" he shouted, boldly striding toward the pit, pretending to act more like a chief in order to buy himself more time.

He frowned and shook his head as the Pelegostos stared. "Not big enough!" he said, widening his arms. *"I am the chief! I need more wood! Big fire!"* he said in the language of the Pelegostos. "MORE WOOD!"

The warriors dropped their spears and hurried away to find wood enough to satisfy their chief. Jack stood tall, his arms folded over his chest, and glowered until every warrior was gone. Then he took off like a shot.

Stumbling across a bridge of twisted vines, he ran past a group of huts. Suddenly finding himself at the edge of a steep cliff and about to fall right over, Jack began waving his arms in a panic. Righting himself, he ran to the nearest hut.

"Rope, long rope," he said, rummaging frantically through the uninhabited hut.

He found a box of spices with the East India Trading Company insignia on it. Jack was about to toss it aside when a huge warrior appeared in the hut's door. Jack stepped back and looked into the warrior's fearsome face.

"Not running away, nooo . . ." Jack said, opening the box of spices. He took a handful and rubbed it on his body. "See?"

Jack soon found himself dusted nicely with a coating of fresh spices and tied to the enormous spit hanging over a huge pile of kindling wood set in a large pit. He sighed and looked down at the fire pit, which now, thanks to his own efforts, was huge. "Nice job," he said, nodding to the proud warriors. Too nice, he added silently to himself.

Meanwhile, inside their cages, the pirates waited helplessly. But Will Turner wasn't about to give up. Elizabeth's life was at stake—he had to get to Jack. "Swing your cage," he yelled to the men as he shifted his weight from side to side, causing the cage to rock. "Get to the wall!"

Leech and the pirates in the other cage got the idea. They rocked their cage to the side of the steep chasm wall and grabbed a vine. "Put your feet through," Will shouted. "Start to climb!"

Pulling with all their might and grabbing for footholds, the crew members slowly moved the two cages up the wall.

A guard passed and stared at the tilted cages for a moment. Every man instantly froze. But after a moment, Leech's men grew anxious and they tried to cheat up an inch. The guard noticed. With a loud scream he sent out the alarm. The drums stopped.

Inside the village, Jack, tied up like a turkey, heard the alarm just as a torch was about to light the pit. The guard suddenly burst into the village, screaming and pointing to the jungle. His meaning was clear—the prisoners were escaping!

"*After them!*" Jack ordered, still trying to appear in charge. He jerked his head toward the jungle. "*Don't let them get away!*"

The warriors hesitated, not knowing whether to light the fire or run. After all, it was their duty to release their god from his fleshy prison. But it was also their god that was commanding them to leave. They finally ran off, tossing the torch to the ground as they left.

Jack's eyes grew wide as the torch slowly rolled toward the pit beneath him. Suddenly, a twig at the edge of the pit caught fire. As the entire pit went up in flames with a giant *whoosh*, Jack tried to blow out the fire. But it was no use. Captain Jack Sparrow was as good as cooked!

Chapter 11

Meanwhile, back in the chasm, Will's cage reached the top first. In the other cage, Leech reached for a thick vine, but screamed as the vine came twisting *into* the cage. Leech had pulled a giant snake, not a vine, into the cage! The pirates quickly let go, and the vine that had been holding them snapped from the weight of the jerking motion. The cage plummeted to the floor of the deep chasm with a crash!

Will heard the men's screams just as he rolled his cage up and out of the chasm. But he didn't have time to worry about Leech and the others. The warriors were racing straight toward his own cage.

With no way to escape, Will and the others pulled the cage up around their legs and began to run through the jungle with their feet sticking out the bottom. They had to get to the *Pearl*. Fast!

* * *

Back in the village, Jack was trying to move fast, too. He was desperately trying to bounce the spit up and down and completely away from the fire. A boy from the village watched as the bouncing pirate choked and sputtered over the flames.

Jack finally bounced high enough and managed to fall away from the pit, gasping for air. He managed to stand upright and ran with the spit on his back as fast as his scorched feet would allow.

The boy who had witnessed Jack's escape ran into the jungle. He caught up to the warriors and told them that Jack had hopped away. The raging warriors howled and took off again . . . but now they weren't after Jack's crew—they were after Jack himself!

Not far away, Will and his portion of the crew had broken free from their cage and had arrived on the beach to find the *Pearl* already prepared. While the warriors had been busy chasing everyone around the island, Pintel and Ragetti had been getting ready to steal the ship. Lucky for Jack's crew, that meant for a fast getaway.

Gibbs was the first aboard. "Excellent!" he called out, seeing the *Black Pearl* ready to make sail. "Our work's half done."

The crew barged past Pintel and Ragetti without a second look and took their spots on deck. "Boys, make ready for sail!" Gibbs shouted.

Will worked alongside Gibbs. "What about Jack? I won't leave without him."

Gibbs suddenly pointed to the beach in horror. Will looked up and saw Jack racing down the beach with a hoard of warriors at his heels.

"Jack! Hurry!" Gibbs shouted. Jack *was* hurrying. The wily captain had managed to get free of the spit. With his arms flailing about, he was trying to stay ahead of the warriors.

Gibbs turned to the crew. "Cast off! Cast off!"

Onshore, the Prison Dog, which had made it to dry land after abandoning Pintel and Ragetti, appeared and began growling at the warriors.

"Good doggy!" Jack shouted, running right by him. Jack sloshed through the surf to the side of the *Pearl*, and Gibbs quickly hauled him aboard.

The dog barked, holding the warriors at bay until the *Black Pearl* disappeared into the horizon. Suddenly, the dog seemed to sense it was in trouble. It stopped barking, wagged its tail a few times, looked at the warriors—the very hungry warriors—then turned and made a run for it.

Chapter 12

Jack Sparrow sat on the deck of the *Black Pearl*, catching his breath.

"Put as much distance between us and this island and make for open sea?" Gibbs asked him.

"Yes to the first and yes to the second, but only insofar as we keep to the shallows . . ." Jack replied, still panting.

Gibbs frowned. "That seems a bit contradictory, sir."

Jack nodded. "I have every faith in your reconciliatory navigational skills, Mr. Gibbs," Jack said, matter of factly.

Then he moved to the rail, opened his Compass, and stared at its face. He was so focused, he didn't notice he had company. Will Turner stood right beside him.

"Jack," Will said quietly.

"Not now," Jack answered, without looking up.

"Jack, I need . . ."

"Not *now*," Jack snapped reaching for his pistol. Finally he looked up at Will. ". . . Oh. You," he said. "Where's that monkey?" Jack asked, figuring that as long as he had his pistol handy, he might as well practice. High in the rigging, the monkey let out a teasing screech.

"Jack," Will said once again, trying to get the captain's attention. "I need that Compass."

"Why?" Jack asked, taking another look before snapping it shut.

"To rescue Elizabeth," Will said.

Jack shook his head and began to climb the rigging. "That has a familiar ring to it," he said. And he was right. The last time Will had found himself in the company of Jack, it had been when he was trying to rescue Elizabeth. To drive the point home, Jack added, "Have you considered keeping a more watchful eye on her? Maybe just lock her up somewhere?"

"She *is* locked up. In prison. Bound to hang for helping you," Will snapped.

Jack paused for a moment as Will's words sunk in. Then he shrugged and continued to climb. "There comes a time when one must take responsibility for one's mistakes," Jack said as he settled into the ship's crow's nest.

Suddenly, Jack felt the cold touch of steel at his throat. It was Will's sword.

"You will hand it over. Now!" he said, leaning into the crow's nest. "In exchange, you will be granted full pardon and commissioned as a privateer in service to England."

Jack sighed. "I wonder what will my crew think when they see you've skewered their beloved and duly chosen captain?"

"I think they will see it as an example," Will told him sternly.

"All right," Jack nodded. "You get the Compass, you rescue your bonnie lass. Where's my profit?"

"You get full pardon," Will explained. "Freedom. A commission."

Jack shook his head. "No, accepting those things is what *you* want from *me*. Don't you want to know what *I* want from *you*?"

Will lowered his sword and turned his head away. Nothing was stickier than negotiating with a blasted pirate. "What do you want from me, Jack?" Will said finally, giving in.

"It's quite dangerous . . ." Jack said, cautioning Will. "I will trade you the Compass, if you will recover for me . . ." He fumbled for the small piece of cloth in his pocket. ". . . this."

Will eyed the imprint of the key on the cloth. "So you get my favor *and* the Letters of Marque, as well?" Leave it to Jack Sparrow to come away on the upside of a tricky bargain, Will thought.

Jack nodded. "And you save fair damsel."

"*This* is going to save Elizabeth?" Will said, looking at the cloth.

Jack leaned in toward Will as if the very air were listening. "How much do you know about Davy Jones?" he asked in a whisper.

"Nothing," Will said.

"Yep," Jack said, nodding firmly, "it's going to save Elizabeth."

Chapter 13

Elsewhere on the ocean, a figure slipped silently across the ratline of the *Edinburgh Trader*. It was Elizabeth Swann, still dressed in the clothes of a sailor. She moved toward the light of the captain's cabin, where she could hear voices raised in an argument.

"It's an outrage!" Captain Bellamy complained, looking at the ship's accounts. "Port tariffs, berthing fees, and, heaven help me, *pilotage!*"

"I'm afraid, sir, Tortuga is the only free port left in these waters," the ship's quartermaster offered, knowing the captain was bound to respond.

And respond he did. Bellamy was furious. "A *pirate* port is what you mean! Well, I'm sorry, but an honest sailor I am. I make my living square, and sleep well each night, thank you."

He didn't get to continue. "Sir!" the bursar interrupted, pointing to the cabin window.

"What?" Bellamy demanded angrily. But the bursar was shaking so hard he could only point. The captain turned to see a shadowy white dress float by the cabin window. He ran out onto the dimly lit deck.

"Tell me you do see that," the ship's cook asked, terrified.

"Aye, I do see that," Bellamy answered as he watched the white gown float to the bowsprit. High up in the rigging, Elizabeth secretly pulled the dress along by a fishing line. With a whisk of her arm, she pulled a line that raised the arm of the dress. It pointed to Captain Bellamy, then out to sea. His crew immediately shuffled away from him.

"She wants you to do something," the bursar said.

"Jump overboard?" the quartermaster asked quickly.

Bellamy tossed him a scowl. "She's trying to give a sign!"

Then, on the sea winds, a soft voice whispered, "Tor . . . tu . . . ga."

"Did you hear that?" the cook exclaimed.

"Bur-mu-da?" the bursar said.

"Tobago?" the quartermaster offered.

Suddenly, the ghostly bride raced toward the rail and dropped over the side. As the crew was busy looking overboard, Elizabeth dropped down behind them.

"Look for a sign!" Bellamy shouted to his men.

"There!" the quartermaster said, pointing out to sea. "There it is! There's the sign!"

"That's seaweed," a sailor pointed out.

"Seaweed can be a sign," the quartermaster argued.

Elizabeth lost all patience. She grabbed the shoulder of the bursar and turned him around. "What's that over there?" she said in a low, deep voice.

On the deck, the word "Tortuga" was burning in lamp oil.

"Is it telling us to go there?" the terrified quartermaster asked.

Elizabeth was about to burst with frustration, when Captain Bellamy spoke up. "Men," he said. "What say ye to a course change? Prudence suggests we make way for the island of Tortuga!"

As the crew shouted their approval, Elizabeth pulled her sailor's cap down lower over her face and smiled. Her plan had worked. Now, all she could do was wait.

Chapter 14

Elizabeth was headed to Tortuga to find Will, but Will was nowhere near Tortuga. He was with Jack Sparrow, headed inland.

Through a heavy mist, two longboats from the *Black Pearl* rowed to the mouth of the Pantano River. Will, Ragetti, and Gibbs rode in the lead, followed by Jack, Pintel, and Cotton. Next to Cotton was a cage covered with a length of canvas.

As they rowed past thick tangles of twisted roots and bark, Will quietly asked Gibbs the question the whole crew wanted to know, "What is it that has Jack so spooked?"

Gibbs heaved a sigh. "Jack has run afoul of none other than Davy Jones himself," he said gravely. "Thinks he is only safe on land. If he goes out to open water, he'll be taken."

"By Davy Jones?" Will asked in disbelief. Jack never seemed scared of anyone.

"Well, I'll tell ye. If you believe such things, there's a beast does the bidding of Davy Jones. A fearsome creature from the depths, with giant tentacles that'll suction your face clean off, and drag an entire ship down to the crushing darkness. The Kraken," Gibbs said, shuddering at the very naming of the evil thing. "They say the stench of its breath . . ." Gibbs stopped, not wanting to go on, and Will could see real fear in the old pirate's eyes. "If you believe such things," he repeated with a tilt of his head and kept rowing.

Will glanced back at Jack, who was nervously working at a hangnail. "Never thought Jack the type to be afraid of dying."

"Aye, but with Jones, it ain't about the dying—it's about the punishment," Gibbs answered. "Think of the worst fate you can conjure for yourself, stretching on forever . . . and that's what awaits you in Davy Jones's locker."

For a moment, everyone on the longboat was silent as they pondered Gibbs's words.

"And the key will spare him that?" Will finally asked.

"Now, that's the very question Jack wants

answered," Gibbs whispered, looking over at the captain. "Bad enough, even, to go visit . . . *her*."

"Her?" Will said nervously.

"Aye," Gibbs nodded.

As the boats rowed into the still water of a steamy bayou, fireflies flickered in the heavy air. The longboats pulled up to a rope ladder that hung down from a sprawling wooden shack high up in a tree. A lantern hung at the door, casting a dim glow on the cautious pirate crew. They had arrived. Now the question was, where?

"No worries, mates," Jack said, trying to sound lighthearted. He grabbed the ladder. "I'll handle this. Tia Dalma and I go way back. Thick as thieves. Nigh inseparable, we were, uh, have been . . . before."

"I'll watch your back," Gibbs volunteered.

"It's me front I'm worried about," Jack muttered.

With one last nervous glance around, Jack pushed his way into the shack, the rest of his crew sticking close behind. As their eyes adjusted to the low light, they saw all manner of strange creatures in jars and bottles. Some were stuffed and hanging from the rafters. Others moved around in jars of murky water. Overhead dangled an old dusty crocodile. Ragetti noticed a jar of eyeballs in a corner and put a hand over his eye socket that was plugged with a wooden eyeball.

At a table, in the shadows, sat Tia Dalma, a mystic with an eye keener than any pirate's. She'd been hovering over crab claws when her head suddenly snapped up. She stood. "Jack Sparrow," she said, "I always knew the wind was going to blow you back to me one day."

Her eyes moved past Jack and landed on Will. She smiled as she looked at him. "You have a touch of destiny in you, William Turner," she said, moving closer.

"You know me?" Will asked, confused.

"You want to know me," she replied in riddle, staring into Will's eyes.

"There will be no knowing here," Jack announced, walking over to Tia Dalma and ushering her back toward the table. "We came here for help."

As the pirates gathered around the table, Tia Dalma pulled Will in close. "Asking for help does not sound like Jack Sparrow."

"It's not so much for me," Jack answered

coolly, "as for William, so he can earn a favor from me."

Tia Dalma nodded. "Now *that* sounds like Jack Sparrow. What service may I do you? You know I demand payment."

"I brought payment!" Jack said brightly, taking the cage from Pintel's hand. He raised the canvas revealing "Jack" the monkey trapped inside. Jack raised his pistol and shot it. The angry little monkey barely blinked. He just glared back.

"See?" Jack exclaimed. He glanced up at the ceiling. "Perhaps you can give it the crocodile treatment?"

Tia Dalma stood and opened the cage.

Gibbs moaned as the monkey raced through the shack. "You don't know how long it took us to catch that," he said sadly.

"The payment is fair," she said, ignoring Gibbs. Her eyes wandered again to Will.

Jack produced the drawing of the key from his pocket and passed it to Will, who quickly showed it to Tia Dalma. "We're looking for this . . . and what it goes to," Will said.

"That Compass you bartered from me can't lead you to this?" Tia Dalma asked.

"No," Jack answered flatly.

Tia Dalma laughed and turned her attention back to Will as she spoke to Jack. "Your key goes to a chest . . . and it is what lies inside the chest you seek, isn't it?"

"What is inside?" Gibbs asked.

"Gold? Jewels? Unclaimed properties of a valuable nature?" Pintel said hopefully.

"Nothing bad, I hope," Ragetti said, still unnerved by it all.

Chapter 15

Tia Dalma smiled at the pirates that surrounded her, as if they were small children. Then she began to tell her tale. "You know of Davy Jones, yes? A man of the sea, a great sailor until he ran afoul of that which vexes all men."

"What vexes all men?" Will asked her.

She smiled. "What, indeed?"

"The sea," Gibbs said solemnly.

Tia Dalma shook her head, no.

"Sums," Pintel said greedily.

The gypsy shook her head again.

"The dichotomy of good and evil," Ragetti suggested. Everyone in the room looked at the one-eyed pirate and shook their heads no.

"A woman," Jack said, ending the game.

Tia Dalma smiled at the rough pirate. "A woman. He fell in love. It was a woman, as changing and harsh and untamable as the sea. He never stopped loving her, but the pain it caused him was too much to live with . . . but not enough to cause him to die."

They each nodded sadly, understanding the story all too well.

"Exactly *what* did he put into the chest?" Will asked.

Tia Dalma sighed. "It was not worth feeling what small, fleeting joy life brings, he decided, and so he carved out his heart, locked it away in a chest, and hid the chest from the world. The key . . . he keeps with him at all times."

Will nodded, understanding. The key would open the chest that held Jones's heart.

"That was a roundabout way to get to the answer," Jack observed.

"Sauce for the gander, Jack," Tia Dalma replied with a wink.

"You knew this," Will said realizing that Jack made a deal based on more information than he'd been willing to reveal.

"No, I didn't. I didn't know where the key was. . . ." Jack stuttered, interrupting Will's thoughts.

Will rolled his eyes.

"But now we do," Jack said smoothly, "so all that is left is to slip aboard Jones's ship, the *Flying Dutchman*, take the key, and then you can go back to Port Royal and save your bonnie lass."

Jack headed for the door, but before he could open it, Tia Dalma said, "Let me see your hand."

Jack hesitated. Slowly, he unwrapped his palm. Tia Dalma nodded respectfully at the sight of the Black Spot that made Jack a marked man.

Gibbs leaned in and saw the mark, too. Pintel and Ragetti watched the old pirate turn three times and spit for luck. Not knowing why, they did the same, just in case.

They watched Tia Dalma move across the room in her long, ragged dress and climb the stairs. At the top, she opened a great carved door. The sound of the ocean whispered from it. Tia Dalma slowly closed the door and descended the stairway. In her hands she carried a jar she handed to Jack. "Davy Jones cannot make port, cannot step on land, but once every ten years," she said to him. Leaning down, she scooped dirt into the jar. "Land is where you are safe, Jack Sparrow, and so you will carry land with you."

Jack looked into the jar. "This is a jar of dirt," Jack said, unimpressed.

"Yes."

"Is the jar of dirt going to help?" he asked skeptically.

Tia Dalma reached for the jar. "If you don't want it, give it back."

"No!" Jack cried, clutching it to his chest.

"Then it helps," she said, nodding.

Will faced Tia Dalma. "It seems we have a need to find the *Flying Dutchman*," he said. Tia Dalma smiled into his young face, then sat again at her table. Scooping up the crab claws, she tossed them down, casting a spell to reveal the direction. The claws did their job well. The crew was on its way to find Davy Jones.

Chapter 16

The *Black Pearl* sailed to an archipelago in the Caribbean that matched the outline of the claws on Tia Dalma's table. And there, on the shoals, lay a ship, the main deck slanted into the sea.

Under the glow of an old oil lantern, Jack and Gibbs silently stared at the broken vessel.

"That's the *Flying Dutchman*?" Will asked them. "She doesn't look like much."

"Neither do you," Jack snapped. "Don't underestimate her." Then he turned to Will. "What's your plan?" he asked.

"I row over, and search the ship until I find your bloody key," Will retorted.

"If there are crewmen?" Jack asked, testing him.

"I cut down anyone in my path."

Jack smiled. "I like it. Simple and easy to remember."

Will nodded. His eyes traveled to the cloth Jack held tightly in his hand. "I bring you the key, you give me the Compass."

"Yes, and if you do get captured, just say, 'Jack Sparrow sent me to settle his debt,'" Jack ordered. Then he added, "It might save your life."

Will nodded his farewells and climbed over the rail to a waiting longboat.

As Will rowed with his back to the scuttled ship, Jack watched silently. Then he ordered Gibbs to lower the lights.

One by one, the lanterns of the *Black Pearl* went as dark as her black sails. She was all but invisible save the smile of one gold-toothed Captain Jack Sparrow.

Will reached the main deck of the broken ship and lit a lantern of his own. The ship seemed deserted. Bodies of seamen, all dead, were strewn haphazardly across the deck. Will felt his legs go weak as he took in the chaos around him. What had he gotten himself into?

Suddenly, a pulley creaked. Will turned to see a wounded sailor weakly trying to raise a sail.

"Hoist the inner jib. Bring up with a round turn. Captain's orders," the man muttered.

"Sailor, there's no use," Will said. "You've run aground."

But the beaten man kept trying. "No . . . beneath us . . . foul breath . . . waves took Billy and Quentin . . . captain's orders!"

A wave suddenly shook the ship and out of the rigging dropped a dead sailor. Will jumped back as the body hit the deck. On the sailor's back, Will could see round suction marks. He turned the body over. The man's face was gone, completely suctioned off.

The Kraken! Gibbs's description of the sea monster came rushing back to Will.

Will quickly backed away from the body. He looked over the rail in a panic and saw nothing but the rolling blackness of the sea. An eerie calm suddenly settled on the waters. Then, almost as quickly, the wind picked up to a gale. The sea churned white, and rising from the foam like a great whale breaking the surface, came an awesome ship of great power. The *Flying Dutchman*.

Will had been tricked. In order to bait the real *Flying Dutchman*, Jack had sent Will aboard a wrecked vessel. But now the ship—and its captain, Davy Jones, had arrived.

It was unlike any ship Will had ever seen. It was made of pallid wood and bones, and completely covered in items from the sea—coral, shells, seaweed. With a splash, it slammed down into the ocean, the skeleton of a winged female attached to her bow. Will hid himself behind one of the wrecked ship's cannons, but it did him no good.

From the shadows, the *Dutchman's* crew boarded the ship. They were a hideous-looking bunch. Some had scales, while others were covered in barnacles. Will pulled his sword and broke cover. He ran for the longboat, but the *Dutchman's* first mate, a man with a coral-encrusted face named Maccus, stopped him. The rest of the crew soon joined Maccus, surrounding Will.

"Down on your marrowbones and pray!" Greenbeard, the Bo'sun, snarled through the seaweed that covered his face.

For a moment, Will stood frozen by the sight of Jones's crew. But as soon as he regained his wits, he ran his sword through a vat of whale oil and thrust it into his lantern. His sword flamed wildly as he slashed away, searing the crewmen's watery flesh. Will spun around to attack the crew at his back when a pulley hit him squarely in the face and knocked him out cold. He was suddenly defenseless and at the mercy of the crew of the *Flying Dutchman.*

Chapter 17

When he came to, Will was still on the scuttled ship. He was part of a line of sailors, all of them on their knees. Will was the final sailor in this line. He looked off to the side and watched as someone strode on to the deck. It was Davy Jones himself—and he was as terrible as he'd been described.

The captain's dark eyes stared out from behind a long beard of octopus tentacles that moved and curled with a life of their own. He had a claw for a left hand and the fingers on his right extended out in rough tentacles wrapping around an ivory cane. On his head he wore a black hat that resembled devil horns, and one of his legs was nothing but whalebone. With a dark glare, he looked down the line of sailors before him.

"Six men still alive," Maccus stated. "The rest have moved on."

Jones nodded and made his way down the line. "Do you fear death?" Jones asked the ship's helmsman, who appeared to be the most frightened. "I can offer you—an escape," he taunted with a voice that echoed of waves crashing on a distant shore.

"Don't listen to him!" said the chaplain, who was also in the line, clutching his cross.

Jones turned and roared, "Do you not fear death?"

"I'll take my chances, sir."

"Good luck, mate," Jones said with a smirk. He nodded to Greenbeard, who tossed the man overboard.

Jones leaned close to the helmsman. His tentacled beard bristled and twisted. "You cling to the pain of life, and fear death. I offer you the choice. Join my crew . . . and postpone judgment. One hundred years before the mast. Will you serve?"

The helmsman nodded quickly. "I will serve."

Jones smiled and moved down the line. At Will, he stopped and frowned. "You are neither dead nor dying. What is your purpose here?"

"Jack Sparrow sent me," Will replied, "to settle his debt."

Anger rose in Jones's face, the tentacles of his beard turning from pale pink to purple. "Did he, now?" He looked at Will for a long moment. "I am sorely tempted to accept that offer."

Jones turned his head and looked out into the darkness. It was time to take care of a little payment.

Chapter 18

Hidden in darkness on the deck of the *Black Pearl*, Jack Sparrow looked through his spyglass and gasped. Jones was staring straight at him.

As Jack slowly lowered his telescope, Davy Jones suddenly and jarringly appeared right in front of him. The crewmen of the *Flying Dutchman* were also transported to the *Pearl*'s deck, and they quickly surrounded Jack and his crew.

"You have a debt to pay," Jones said to Jack with a nasty growl. "You've been captain of the *Black Pearl* for thirteen years. That was our agreement."

Jack nodded. "Technically, I was only captain for two years—then I was viciously mutinied upon."

"But a captain nonetheless," Jones replied. "Have you not introduced yourself all this time as Captain Jack Sparrow?"

"Not that I recall. Why do you ask? You have my payment. One soul, to serve on your ship. He's already over there," Jack said, referring to Will.

"You can't trade," Jones roared. "You can't substitute."

Jack raised a finger. "There is precedent regarding servitude, according to The Code of the Brethren. . . ."

The tentacles on Jones's face twisted and curled. "One soul is not the same as another!"

"Ah, so we've established the proposal is sound in principle. Now we're just haggling over the price," Jack replied.

"As has been the case before, I am oddly compelled to listen to you," Jones confessed.

Jack saw his chance to bargain and pounced on it. "Just how many souls do you think my soul is worth?" he asked slyly.

Jones pondered. "One hundred souls. Three days," was the reply.

Jack flashed a sparkling grin. "You're a diamond, mate. Send me back the boy, I'll get started, right off."

"I keep the boy. A good-faith payment. That leaves you only ninety-nine more to go."

"What?" Jack asked, astounded. "Have you

met Will Turner? He's noble and heroic, a terrific soprano . . . he's worth at least four. And did I mention he is in love? Due to be married. To a lovely young lady. You hate that malarkey."

Jones was not to be swayed by Jack's fancy words. "I keep the boy," he snapped. "You owe ninety-nine souls. In three days. But I wonder, Sparrow . . . can you live with this?"

Jack considered the question briefly.

"Yep," he answered.

"You can condemn an innocent man—a friend—to a lifetime of servitude, in your name, while you roam free?" Jones asked.

"I'm good with it," Jack answered. "Shall we seal it in blood? I mean, ink?"

"Let's not, and say we did. Agreed?"

"Agreed," Jack said, still grinning. Jack looked down at his palm. The Black Spot was gone. When he looked back up, Davy Jones and his crew were gone, too.

Moments later, the *Flying Dutchman* sailed off into a distant storm with Will aboard. Jack watched silently as the ship faded from sight. He had three days to find ninety-nine souls. There was only one place to go—Tortuga.

Chapter 19

In a corner of a crowded cantina in Tortuga, Jack sat, his feet up, Compass in hand. As Gibbs went about the business of recruiting Jack's much needed ninety-nine souls, Jack drank from a large mug and listened in. An unforgettable journey aboard the *Black Pearl* is what Gibbs promised a line of hopeful sailors. Of course, being as it was Tortuga, every one of them was beaten and broken down.

"I've one arm and a bum leg," an old sailor told Gibbs.

"Crow's nest for you," Gibbs replied. After a few more interviews, Gibbs walked over to Jack.

"How are we doing?" Jack asked, looking up.

"Counting those four?" Gibbs sighed. "That gives us four." Gibbs worried over the number. "Nothing better happen to *me*," he added hastily.

"I make no promises," Jack said, raising an eyebrow. He was not fond of promises.

"You'd best be coming up with a new plan, Jack, and it better not be relying on that Compass. The whole crew knows it ain't worked since you was saved from the gallows."

Jack scowled as Gibbs moved back to the meager line of recruits.

"What's your story?" Gibbs said to the next sailor. The man was drunk and unshaven, but his eyes were clear.

"My story," the man replied. "Same as your story, just one chapter behind. I became obsessed with capturing a notorious pirate . . . chased him across the seven seas. I lost all perspective, I was consumed. The pursuit cost me my crew, my commission, my life."

Gibbs took a closer look at the man. "Commodore?" he asked, suddenly recognizing him. It was Commodore Norrington—the very man who had chased Jack and the *Pearl* all the way to *Isla de Muerta*.

"Not anymore," the former commodore answered. He slammed his bottle down. "So what is it? Do I make your crew, or not?"

Gibbs didn't answer. He was stunned to see the fine commodore turned into a rough gentleman of fortune like himself.

The silence seemed to anger Norrington. "So, am I worthy to serve under Captain Jack Sparrow?" he roared. Then he turned and pulled his pistol. ". . . Or should I just kill you now?" he said, aiming it across the room at Jack, who was trying to sneak away.

Jack froze and quickly forced a smile. "You're hired, mate!"

Norrington pulled the hammer back. "Sorry," he said, about to shoot anyway, "old habits die and all that."

"Easy, soldier," a man said, grabbing Norrington's arm, "that's our captain you be threatening."

A wild shot went off and the man ducked, knocking over a table. Jack's new crew suddenly jumped up and began swinging. Pirates, out for a night of sport, joined in the brawl and swung back, tossing chairs and smashing bottles.

"Time to go," Jack said, nodding to Gibbs.
"Aye."

Jack danced through the brawl without even

a scratch. On his way out he stooped over a man who had been knocked out, and tried on his hat. Too small, Jack decided as he and Gibbs made their way to the cantina's back stairs. It was so hard to find a good hat these days, he thought to himself as the fight waged on.

As Jack and Gibbs slipped quietly away, Norrington was left with his back to a beam slashing at the drunken hoard. "Come on, then. Do you want some British steel? You, you, you?" He was still shouting when a bottle was suddenly smashed over his head, taking him down.

Standing over him, dressed in her sailor's clothing, was Elizabeth. "I just wanted the pleasure of doing that myself," she shouted to the pirates. "Now let's toss this mess out of here and have a drink!"

The pirates roared and tossed Norrington out to the pigs wallowing behind the cantina. Elizabeth suddenly recognized the man. And she couldn't believe her eyes.

Chapter 20

Moments later, Elizabeth rushed to the former commodore's side and knelt down. "James Norrington," she said pitying the poor man. "What has the world done to you?"

"Nothing I didn't deserve," Norrington answered, as Elizabeth helped him to his feet.

Slowly, they made their way to the docks and stepped directly into Jack's path. "Captain Sparrow," Elizabeth said to him.

Jack looked at her. He didn't recognize her in her sailor disguise. "Come to join my crew, lad? Well enough, welcome aboard."

"I've come to find the man I love," Elizabeth declared.

Jack nodded, still not aware he was speaking to Elizabeth.

"I'm deeply flattered, son, but my first and only love is the sea," Jack replied.

"Meaning, William Turner, Captain Sparrow," Elizabeth added stiffly.

"Elizabeth?" Jack said, eyeing her warily. "You know, those clothes do *not* flatter you at all."

"Jack," Elizabeth said, staying focused, "I know Will set out to find you. Where is he?"

"Darling, I am truly unhappy to have to tell you this, but through an unfortunate and entirely unforeseeable series of circumstances that have nothing whatsoever to do with me . . . poor Will was press-ganged into Davy Jones's crew."

"Davy Jones," Elizabeth repeated, not sure if she should believe the pirate.

"Oh, please," Norrington scoffed. "The captain of the *Flying Dutchman*? A ship that ferries those who died at sea from this world to the next . . ."

"Bang on!" Jack exclaimed. Then, recognizing Norrington, he added, "You look bloody awful, mate. What are you doing here?"

"You hired me," was his reply. "I can't help that your standards are lax."

"Jack," Elizabeth said, "all I want is to find Will."

Jack tugged at his beaded black beard for a moment before carefully replying. "Are you certain? Is that what you really want . . . most?"

"Of course," Elizabeth answered. She suddenly saw a gleam in Jack's eyes.

"I'd think you'd want to find a way to save Will . . . most," Jack replied.

"And you have a way to do that?"

"Well," Jack began, ". . . there is a chest. A chest of unknown size and origin."

"What contains the still-beating heart of Davy Jones!" Pintel interjected as he passed, carrying a barrel onto the *Black Pearl*.

"Thump, THUMP!" Ragetti added, patting his hand against his chest with a grin.

Ignoring the scurvy pair, Jack quickly said, "And whoever possesses that chest possesses the leverage to command Jones to do whatever it is he . . . or she . . . wants. Including saving our brave William from his grim fate."

"How can we find it?" Elizabeth asked flatly. She didn't trust Jack, but she wanted to get to Will—soon.

Jack placed the Compass in her hand. "With this. This Compass is unique."

"Unique here having the meaning of 'broken'?" Norrington asked.

Jack tilted his head. "True enough, this Compass does not point north," he said, but then added, "it points to the thing you want most in this world."

Still skeptical, Elizabeth asked, "Jack, are you telling the truth?"

"Every word, luv. What you want most in the world is to find the chest of Davy Jones, is it not?"

Elizabeth nodded. "To save Will."

Jack opened the Compass in her hand. "By finding the chest of Davy Jones," he said for emphasis. Looking at the Compass heading, he turned to Gibbs. "We have our heading!" he shouted. The *Pearl*'s crew was on its way . . . finally.

Chapter 21

Meantime, on the deck of the *Flying Dutchman*, Davy Jones sat playing an organ of coral that seemed to have grown from the organic molding of the deck itself. The tune was sad and haunting and, as the notes drifted over the boat, Jones's eyes misted. His gaze was drawn to the image of a woman with flowing hair that was etched into the coral above the huge keyboard.

Elsewhere on the deck, the crewmembers were hard at work—including one of the newest additions, Will Turner. He was hauling a line when it suddenly slipped through his hands and a boom fell, crashing to the deck.

"Haul the weevil to his feet!" the Bo'sun shouted. In his hands he held a cat-o'-nine-tails. He slapped it against his palm. "Five from the lash'll remind you to stay on 'em!" he said, walking over to Will. But before he could take a swing,

Bootstrap Bill reached out and grabbed the crewman's wrist.

"Impeding me in my duties!" the Bo'sun snarled. "You'll share the punishment!"

"I'll take it all," Bootstrap told him.

"Will you, now?" Davy Jones asked. He had stopped playing the organ and was observing the situation carefully. "And what would prompt such an act of charity?"

Bootstrap lifted a barnacled hand, motioning toward Will. "My son. That's my son."

Jones smiled as he watched Will's eyes widen at the sight of his father. "What fortuitous circumstance be this!" Jones roared, slapping his knee. "You wish to spare your son the Bo'sun's discipline?"

"Aye," Bootstrap answered.

"Give your lash to Mr. Turner. The elder," Jones ordered the Bo'sun.

Bootstrap Bill protested as the lash was placed in his hand. Being forced to lash his own son was the worst possible punishment.

"The cat's out of the bag, Mr. Turner!" Jones roared. The crew cowered. "Your issue will taste its sting, be it by the Bo'sun's hand . . . or your own!"

The Bo'sun went to take back the lash, but Bootstrap pushed him away. He raised the lash to Will, his barnacled arm snapping forward.

Will half staggered to the hold later that night, Bootstrap following behind him. "The Bo'sun prides himself on cleaving flesh from bone with every swing," Bootstrap explained as he helped Will to a bench.

Will stared. He couldn't believe that after all these years, he was finally talking to his father.

"So I'm to understand what you did was an act of compassion?" Will asked his father.

Bootstrap nodded.

"Then I guess I am my father's son. For nearly a year, I've been telling myself that I killed you to save you," Will admitted.

"You killed me?" Bootstrap replied.

"I lifted the curse you were under knowing it would mean your death. But, at least, you would no longer suffer the fate handed to you by Barbossa."

"Who is Barbossa?" Bootstrap asked blankly.

"Captain Barbossa," Will said, wondering how his father's mind could have dulled so as not to remember. "The man who led the mutiny aboard the *Black Pearl*? Who left you to live forever at the bottom of the ocean."

"Oh. Of course," Bootstrap said, nodding. His eyes misted. "It's the gift and the lie given by Jones," he told young Will. "You join the crew and think you've cheated the powers, but it's not reprieval you've found. It's oblivion. Losing what you were, bit by bit, till you end up like poor Wyvern here."

Will followed his father's eyes and noticed what looked like a carved image of an old sailor, his body part of the ship's hull.

Bootstrap sighed. "Once you've sworn an oath to the *Dutchman*, there's no leaving it. Not till your debt is paid. By then, you're not just on the ship, but of it. Why did you do it, Will?"

"I've sworn no oath," Will said truthfully.

Bootstrap's face brightened at the news. "Then you must get away."

"Not until I find this," Will said showing his father the image of the key. "It's supposed to be on the ship. Jack wanted it; maybe it is a way out?"

Suddenly, old Wyvern moved, pulling himself free from the hold of the hull's wood. "The

Captain Jack is back for another adventure on
the high seas.

Elizabeth Swann's wedding day is ruined.

Lord Beckett has put Elizabeth in jail, and Will promises he will rescue her.

Will Turner sails off to find Captain Jack Sparrow.

Will is captured by warriors.

The warriors have a new leader—Captain Jack!

Elizabeth Swann disguises herself as a sailor.

Will listens while Tia Dalma tells them
the story of Davy Jones.

Jack sneaks away. He needs to leave
Tortuga and find Jones's chest.

Davy Jones captains the *Flying Dutchman*.

Will shows his father, Bootstrap Bill,
a picture of Davy Jones's key.

Pirates Pintel and Ragetti have stolen
Davy Jones's chest!

Dead Man's Chest!" he moaned, his arms reaching for the cloth.

Will jumped back as the wooden creature, who had torn himself away from the body of the ship, opened his mouth and wailed. Will blanched. He knew this was the fate for all who served Davy Jones. Old Bootstrap would soon fade into the hull, too. One more tormented soul to become part of the ship itself. But Wyvern's next words gave Will hope.

"Open the chest with the key, and stab the heart," old Wyvern cried, then seemed to suddenly change his mind. "Don't stab the heart! The *Dutchman* must have a living heart or there is no captain! And if there is no captain, there's no one to have the key!"

"The captain has the key?" Will asked, confused by Wyvern's ravings.

"Hidden," was all Wyvern said and withdrew, once again becoming one with the hull of the ship.

But Will had his answer—and that was half of what he needed.

The key was with Jones.

Will headed for the deck.

Chapter 22

Aboard the *Black Pearl*, Jack Sparrow found Elizabeth filling in the names on the Letters of Marque that she'd taken from Lord Beckett.

Jack immediately snatched them away. "These Letters of Marque are supposed to go to *me*, are they not?"

Jack spotted the signature on the papers. "Lord Cutler Beckett. *He's* the man wants my Compass?"

Elizabeth hesitated. "Not the Compass, a chest."

The word caught Gibbs's attention. "A chest? Not the chest of Davy Jones? If the East India Trading Company controls the chest, they'll control the sea," Gibbs grumbled.

Elizabeth's ears perked up—control of the sea. So *that* was why Beckett was so eager to get his hands on the chest! It had nothing to do with Jack. She turned her attention back to the captain.

"Aye, a discomforting notion," the captain agreed. "May I inquire as to how you came by these?"

"Persuasion," Elizabeth answered.

Jack raised an eyebrow. "Friendly?" he asked with a smile.

"Decidedly not," Elizabeth snapped. She didn't have time for Jack's games . . . or his flirting.

Jack scowled and looked again at the letters. "Full pardon," he huffed. "Commission as a privateer on behalf of England and the East India Trading Company. As if I could be bought." He shook his head and stuffed the letters in his jacket pocket. "Not for this low of a price. Fate worse than death, living a life like that . . ."

"Jack," Elizabeth said. "The letters. Give them back."

Jack looked at her. "Persuade me," he said with a grin.

Elizabeth hesitated, then turned her back on the infuriating pirate who was smugly patting the Letters in his jacket pocket. Norrington had been standing nearby, listening in. As she passed by him to leave, he couldn't help but notice a small smile playing on her face.

"It's a curious thing," Norrington said, falling into step with Elizabeth. "There was a time when I'd have given anything for you to look like that while thinking of me. Just once."

Elizabeth stiffened at the suggestion that she might have an interest in Captain Jack. "I don't know what you mean," Elizabeth said.

"I think you do," Norrington insisted.

"Don't be absurd. I trust him, that's all."

"Ah," Norrington nodded. He turned to walk away, but not without one final thought to leave with Elizabeth.

"Did you never wonder how your fiancé ended up on the *Flying Dutchman* in the first place?" Norrington asked.

Chapter 23

Back on the *Dutchman,* Will had made his way to the main deck. A game of Liar's Dice was being played by a few of the crew.

Standing back a bit, Will observed the game and tried to follow along.

"I wager ten years!" Maccus said hotly.

Another crewman matched the ten years and the game was on. Each man bid a number, then Maccus peeked at the dice under his cup. "Four fives," he said firmly.

"Liar!" another crewman in the game called. Maccus cursed as he revealed his dice. The barnacled sea man had only three fives.

"What are they playing for?" Will asked Bootstrap, who had followed his son.

"The only thing any of us has," Bootstrap sighed, "years of service."

"Any member of the crew can be challenged?"

Will asked his father thoughtfully.

"Aye," Bootstrap replied.

"I challenge Davy Jones," Will boldly announced.

The crew went silent and, as if by magic, Jones appeared instantly on the deck. "Accepted," he told Will, eyeing him carefully. "But I only bet for what's dearest to a man's heart."

"I wager a hundred years of service," was Will's reply.

"No!" Bootstrap cried.

"Against your freedom?" Jones asked.

"My father's freedom." Will thought he had no need to wager against his own freedom. He thought he was already free, having no idea Jack had been bargaining with his soul.

"Agreed," Jones answered and took a seat across from Will. Jones eagerly rolled first. "You are a desperate man," Jones remarked. "You are the one who hopes to get married. But your fate is to be married to this ship."

"I choose my own fate," Will replied.

"Then it wouldn't be fate, would it?" Jones answered. "Five threes."

Will took a breath. "Five sixes," he said.

Jones looked in his eyes. "Liar."

Will revealed his dice. To the crew's shock, he had five sixes! "Well done, Master Turner," Jones said, rising to leave. Will had won the first round. His father was free.

But Will wasn't satisfied. "Another game," he said suddenly.

The crew gasped. "You can't best the devil twice, son," Jones said, cautioning him.

Will smiled knowingly. "Then why are you walking away?"

Jones's beard curled wildly. He didn't like to be goaded.

"The stakes?" Jones asked, taking his seat again.

"I wager my soul," Will answered. "An eternity of servitude."

"Against?" Jones asked.

"What was it you said about that which is dearest to a man's heart?" Will asked, presenting the cloth. "I want this."

Jones heaved his huge head. "How do you know of the key?" he snarled.

"That's not part of the game, is it?" Will asked.

Jones scowled as one of his tentacles

reached into his shirt and pulled out the key. It hung from a chain Jones wore around his neck. That's what Will needed to see. He now knew where the key was hidden, and he tried not to show his satisfaction. He slammed his cup down along with Jones's, when another cup suddenly slammed down, too.

"I'm in," Bootstrap said looking at Jones. "Matching his wager, an eternity in service to you." Not waiting for permission, Bootstrap began a new game. "I bid three twos," he said, looking at his dice under the cup.

"Don't do this," Will begged.

Too much was at stake now that his father was playing. If Will lost, he would join Jones's crew, but at least his father would be free. But if Bootstrap lost, he would again be bound to the ship, even though Will would go free.

"The die's been cast, Will. Your bid, Captain," Bootstrap said, ignoring his son's pleas.

Davy Jones checked his dice. "Four threes."

"Five threes," Will said reluctantly.

"Seven fives," Jones told them.

Will couldn't go any higher. "Eight fives," he said, bluffing.

Jones smiled. He knew Will was lying. "Welcome to the crew, lad."

"Twelve fives," Bootstrap yelled suddenly. Jones glowered at him, but Bootstrap held steady. "Call me a liar, or up the bid."

Jones slipped the key back into his shirt. "Bootstrap Bill, you are a liar, and you will spend an eternity of service to me on this ship. William Turner . . . feel free to go ashore . . . the very next time we make port." Jones laughed and moved off.

Will was furious. "You fool! Why did you do that?"

Bootstrap dropped his tired head and said, "I couldn't let you lose."

"It was never about winning or losing," Will said, sighing. Bootstrap stared at him for a moment, then suddenly understood . . . it was about finding the key. And Will had, at least, done that.

Chapter 24

Later that night, the merchant ship, the *Edinburgh Trader*, appeared on the horizon near the *Dutchman*. Grabbing Will, Bootstrap went to the railing and quietly pointed the *Trader* out to Will. "It's your chance," Bootstrap whispered.

Will nodded. But before he could get on the passing ship, he had something to take care of. He moved toward the captain's cabin and quietly slipped inside. Jones was asleep, sprawled across the organ. Will moved a step closer when Jones's finger suddenly hit a key. The noise echoed through the cabin, but the sleeping captain didn't move. Will held his breath and crept up to the organ. Pushing away Jones's tentacled beard, he reached for the key.

Just as Will worked it off the chain, a single tentacle grabbed the key and tried to pull it back to Jones. Will looked down at the cloth that he still held in his hand. He rolled it up and quickly placed the cloth in the tentacle's grip. Satisfied to be holding something, the tentacle released the key and rested peacefully again with the cloth in its clutches.

Will retreated from the cabin and dashed back to Bootstrap. "Is she still there?" he asked, his eyes searching the dark sea for the *Trader*.

Bootstrap had readied a longboat for Will. "Aye, but the moment's slipping away."

Will's heart ached to leave his father behind. He climbed over the side of the *Dutchman*. "Come with me," he pleaded.

"I can't. I'm part of the ship now, Will. I can't leave. Take this," he said, handing him a black knife from his belt. "Always meant for you to have it . . ."

Will smiled. "I will see you free of this prison. I promise you."

Will slipped into the longboat and disappeared on the dark waters of the night.

The next morning, a large crewman arrived to take Bootstrap's place on watch. He found the old pirate asleep and kicked him hard. "Show a leg, before the captain spots you."

Suddenly, the crewman's eyes fell on the white sails of the *Edinburgh Trader*. "All hands!" he bellowed. "Ship a quarter stern!"

Davy Jones came on deck and looked out to sea. "Who stood watch last night?"

The crew pushed Bootstrap forward. "How is it, Bootstrap, you let a ship pass by, unnoticed?" the tentacled captain asked.

"Beggin' your mercy, Capt'n, I fell sound asleep. Beggin' your mercy, it won't happen again."

"Bring the son," Jones ordered.

"He's not onboard, sir," a crewman said. "One of the longboats is missing."

Jones immediately understood. He met Bootstrap's eye and watched the pirate's face grow pale. Jones pulled the chain from his shirt. The key was gone. There was only one person tricky enough to be behind this. "Jack Sparrow," he shouted. "Captain Jack Sparrow!"

Chapter 25

In the captain's cabin of the *Edinburgh Trader*, Will huddled underneath a blanket and clutched a warm drink in his hand. As he tried to thaw out, Captain Bellamy tried to understand what was going on. "Strange thing, to come upon a long-boat so far out in open waters," he said.

"Just put as many leagues behind us as you can, as fast as you can," Will replied. His eyes fell on Elizabeth's wedding dress thrown casually across a chair.

"That dress. Where did you get it?" Will asked.

"Funny, that dress," Captain Bellamy said. "Found aboard the ship. Put quite a stir into the crew, thought it was a spirit, bringing an omen of ill fate. But it brought good fortune! The spirit told us, put in at Tortuga, and we made a nice bit of profit there . . . off the books."

Will ran his fingers over the white fabric and smiled. "I imagine some of your crew might have jumped ship there?"

"Bound to happen," Bellamy said with a wave of his hand.

A sailor on deck suddenly rushed to the cabin. "Captain! A ship's been spotted!"

"Colors?" Bellamy asked.

"She's not flying any, sir," the sailor replied.

"Pirates," Bellamy said, glancing warily at Will.

"Or worse," Will cried, rushing out on to the deck. He climbed the yard arm and looked out at the water.

"It's the *Dutchman!*" Will cried. "I've doomed us all."

Will had barely finished speaking when the *Edinburgh Trader* lurched to a sudden stop. "Mother Cary's chickens!" the bursar shouted in alarm. "What happened?"

"Must have hit a reef," the quartermaster answered. After all, large ships did not just stop on their own accord.

Captain Bellamy looked over the rail, trying to see what had halted them. The sea looked empty. "Free the rudder!" he commanded. "Hard to port, then starboard, and back again!"

The sailors followed orders and turned for more instructions. But Bellamy was gone. The crew looked out toward the sea, where what appeared to be a tiny figure was wrapped in a huge tentacle. As the crew looked closer, it was clear to them that the figure was the captain! The tentacle rose high in the air and then slapped the screaming captain down upon the water.

"KRAKEN!" the crew shouted in terror.

Having taken out the captain, the Kraken came back for the ship. The arms of the huge creature swept over the deck and smashed the longboats.

In a spray of wood and sea foam, the Kraken broke the ship in two and pulled it under.

When it was over, six men kneeled on the deck of the *Flying Dutchman*. "Where is the son?" Jones asked, studying the line of terrified sailors. "And where is the key?"

"No sign," Maccus answered. "He must have been claimed by the sea."

"I *am* the sea!" Jones bellowed angrily.

"Overboard," he shouted motioning to the doomed sailors. They were of no use to him.

As his crewman tossed the last survivors of the merchant ship over the side, Jones paced the deck. "The chest is no longer safe," he growled, knowing that Bootstrap's son had the key, and he also knew Will was working with Jack. "Crowd on sail, and gather way. Chart a course to *Isla Cruces.*"

"He won't find the chest," a crewman said.

"He knew about the key, didn't he?" Jones shouted impatiently. He would not risk Jack discovering the location of his heart. He needed to get to *Isla Cruces* before Will—or Jack—arrived. "Get me there first," Jones shouted. "Or there be the devil to pay!"

Holding fast to the stern of the *Dutchman* and able to hear every word on deck, the sole survivor of the *Edinburgh Trader*, Will Turner, now knew where the chest was hidden. Hunkering down on the stern, he was suddenly filled with hope. He had a ride to the chest . . . and the key in his pocket!

Chapter 26

While Will was hitching a ride to *Isla Cruces* on the *Dutchman*, Jack headed for the same island on the *Black Pearl*. Jack's Compass, in Elizabeth's hand, had finally given him proper direction.

But Elizabeth didn't seem very happy.

"Elizabeth, are you well? Everything ship-shape and Bristol fashion? My tremendous intuitive sense of the female creature informs me you are troubled," Jack gallantly said.

Elizabeth let out a sigh. "I just thought I'd be married by now," she said.

Jack smiled agreeably. "I like marriage! It's like a wager on who will fall out of love first."

Elizabeth moved away, but Jack pursued her. "You know, I am captain of a ship. I could perform a marriage right here on this deck, right now."

"No, thank you," Elizabeth said to his hasty proposal.

"Why not?" he asked her, smiling. "Admit it, we are so much alike, you and I. I and you."

"Except for a, oh, a sense of decency and honor," Elizabeth said. "And a moral center. And personal hygiene."

Jack looked himself over. "Trifles!" he said quickly. "You will come over to my side, in time. I know."

"You seem quite certain."

Jack nodded. "One word, luv. Curiosity. You long for freedom. To do what you want because you want it. To act on selfish impulse. You want to see what it's like. Someday," he said, looking into her eyes, "you won't be able to resist."

Elizabeth's expression was stonelike. With a chill in her voice, she replied, "Because you and I are alike, there will come a moment when you have the chance to show it—to do the right thing."

Jack brightened. "I love those moments! I like to wave as they pass by!"

Elizabeth ignored him. "You will have a chance to do something brave," she told him. "And in that moment you will discover something."

Jack looked at her as if he couldn't imagine

what on earth that something might be. He looked puzzled, as if he were trying to figure it out.

"That you are a good man!" Elizabeth told him, finally.

"All evidence to the contrary," Jack pointed out.

"I have faith in you. Do you know why? Curiosity," she said confidently. "You're going to want it. A chance to be admired and gain the rewards that follow. You won't be able to resist."

Jack opened his mouth to retort but was stopped by a loud command, "Land, ho!"

Jack raced to the rail. He could see the tiny island of *Isla Cruces* on the horizon. He stared down into the suddenly still water. The island was too far away for Jack's taste. "I want my jar," he said meekly.

Chapter 27

Captain Jack Sparrow sat in a longboat, clutching his jar of dirt like a frightened child. Opposite him were Elizabeth and Norrington, both trying to take seriously what they saw as the captain's ridiculous behavior. Pintel and Ragetti were rowing the longboat toward *Isla Cruces*.

"You're pulling too fast," Pintel complained to his one-eyed friend.

"You're pulling too slow," Ragetti answered. "We don't want the Kraken to catch us."

Jack cringed at the mention of the sea monster's name.

"I'm saving me strength for when it comes," Pintel said. "And I don't think it's 'Krack-en,' anyways. I always heard it said 'Kray-ken.'"

Jack cringed again. "What, with a long *a*? Krock-en's how it is in the original Scandinavian,"

Ragetti answered, leaning on the oars. "And Krack-en's closer to that."

They heard a sudden splash in the water and the two took to rowing faster. They could debate later.

Reaching the shore, Jack gratefully hopped out. He took off his jacket, patted the pocket to make sure the Letters of Marque were still there, placed it and the jar in the longboat's bow, and grabbed a shovel. "Guard the boat. Mind the tide," he ordered Pintel and Ragetti. Jack thrust the Compass into Elizabeth's hands and they made their way up the beach.

"I didn't expect anyone to be here," Norrington said when they came upon an abandoned church.

"There's not," Elizabeth answered.

"You know this place?" he asked, surprised.

"Stories," Elizabeth said, moving on. "The Church came to the island, and brought salvation, and disease and death. They say the priest had to bury everybody, one after the other. It drove him mad, and he hung himself."

"Better mad with the rest of the world than sane alone," Norrington noted. Elizabeth stared at him. Norrington had changed so much since she first met him. This cynical man was not the commodore she had once known.

"No fraternizing with the help, love," Jack said, interrupting her thoughts. Elizabeth scowled, looked down at the Compass and continued to walk. Suddenly, the needle began to swing wildly—they had found the spot! Jack drew an *X* in the sand with the toe of his boot and handed the shovel to Norrington.

At the same time, on an outer reef of *Isla Cruces*, the *Flying Dutchman* came around the point. Through his spyglass, Davy Jones saw the longboat. "They're here," he scowled, stomping the deck. "And I cannot step foot on land again for near of a decade!"

"Ye'll trust us to act in yer stead?" Maccus asked him.

"I trust you to know what awaits should you fail!" Jones promised. "Down, then," he ordered his crew.

Maccus nodded and called out, "Down, down." The bow of the *Flying Dutchman* submerged into the blue sea, bubbles rushing over her deck. In a moment, the entire ship went under and moved beneath the waves as swiftly as if it were being pushed down by a huge, invisible hand. Fish darted by as the *Dutchman* headed, beneath the waves, for *Isla Cruces*, churning the sea above her to foam.

Sitting on the beach, Pintel and Ragetti stared out at the boiling sea and turned to each other in terror. Springing to their feet, they left the longboat and ran to warn the others.

Chapter 28

Time was running out for Jack. He and Elizabeth stood anxiously over the hole Norrington had dug. They gave a start when the shovel suddenly clanked against something hard. They had hit the chest! Jack jumped in the hole and helped lift it out.

Jack quickly broke the lock with the shovel. He sank to his knees and opened the chest. Inside were the mementos of a love lost; a strand of white pearls and a long white dress, dried flowers, and faded love letters. Jack pushed the stuff aside— and found a box. He lifted the box from the chest. It was bound in bands of iron and locked tightly, but the sound of a single deep beat could be heard coming from inside.

"It's real!" Elizabeth gasped.

Norrington was astounded. "You actually were telling the truth."

Jack raised an eyebrow. "I do that a lot, and yet people are still surprised."

"With good reason," came a voice.

The group turned to see Will Turner. He approached them, out of breath and soaked to the skin.

With a gasp of astonishment, Elizabeth rushed to him. "Will—you're all right!" She threw her arms around his neck.

Jack looked behind Will, worriedly. "How did you get here?" he asked Will.

"Sea turtles, mate. A pair of them, strapped to my feet," Will said, referencing a well-known legend that Jack Sparrow himself had escaped an island on the backs of turtles.

Jack grinned at Will's slight. "Not so easy, is it?"

"But I do owe you thanks, Jack," Will said. "After you tricked me onto that ship—to square your debt to Jones . . ."

"What?" Elizabeth said, looking at Jack.

". . . I was reunited with my father."

Jack gulped. "You're welcome."

"Everything you said to me . . . *every word* was a lie?" Elizabeth said, glaring at Jack.

"Yes. Time and tide, love," Jack nodded with no apology. Then the cocky expression left his face as he noticed Will kneeling beside the chest. Will had the key in one hand, the knife his father had given him in the other.

"What are you doing?" Jack asked.

"I'm going to kill Jones," Will answered.

In a flash, a cool blade was pressed against Will's throat. It was Jack's blade.

"I can't let you do that, William," Jack said. "If Jones is dead, then who's to call his beastie off the hunt? Now, if you please—the key."

Quick as lightning, Will slapped Jack's sword away, jumped back, and grabbed the cutlass Elizabeth had been carrying since her trip to Tortuga. "I keep the promises I make," he said, facing off with Jack. "I intend to free my father."

But suddenly, Norrington drew his sword and turned it on Will. "I can't let you do that, either. Sorry."

Jack looked at the former commodore and grinned. "I knew you'd warm up to me eventually," he said, delighted with the sudden turn of events.

Norrington pointed his sword quickly toward Jack, and revealed his true intention. "Lord Beckett desires the contents of that chest. If I deliver it, I get my life back."

"Ah, the dark side of ambition," Jack sighed grimly.

The three men instantly sprung forward, their swords all locked together in a clash of steel.

"Will," Jack said urgently, "we can't let him get the chest. You can trust me on this!" Will held his sword steady, his eyes wide with disbelief. "You can mistrust me less than you can mistrust him," Jack finally offered.

Will stopped to consider, then looked at Norrington. "You look awful," he said to the bedraggled commodore.

"Granted," Norrington replied. "But you're still naïve. Jack just wants Elizabeth for himself."

"Pot. Kettle. Black," Jack said, summing up the situation in three words.

The three men sprung back, clashing swords again.

"Guard the chest," Will told Elizabeth as he, Norrington, and Jack swung wildly at each other.

"No! This is barbaric! This is not how grown men settle their affairs!" Elizabeth shouted. They paid her no attention.

From between the palms, Ragetti, who had made it safely off the beach, had been watching the scene. "Now, how'd this a-go all screwy?" Pintel asked, arriving beside him and crouching low. They both eyed the chest.

Ragetti sighed. "Each wants the chest for hisself. Mr. Norrington, I think, is hopin' to regain a bit of honor, ol' Jack's looking to trade it to save his own skin, and Turner there . . . he's tryin' to settle some unresolved business 'twixt him and his twice-cursed pirate father."

"Sad," Pintel commented. "That chest must be worth more'n a shiny penny. If we was any kind of decent, we'd remove temptation from their path." The two pirates gave each other a sideways glance, and crept toward the chest.

Elizabeth was still trying to stop the wild sword fight, but nothing seemed to help. She fell to the sand, pretending to faint in the hopes that the men would halt their battle and help her. She lay still as long as she could, then opened her eyes in time to catch Pintel and Ragetti making off into the jungle with the chest.

Jumping to her feet, she was torn for a moment between telling Will or chasing the chest. She squinted as she saw the three men slashing away at each other in the distance, and decided to duck into the jungle and go after the pirates.

Chapter 29

The fight was in full swing and moving all over the island.

Norrington shoved Will back hard and the key was dropped.

"Hah-hah!" Jack howled, watching the key launch into the air before landing squarely in his hand. Norrington and Will stood stunned as Jack took off down the beach with the key, then quickly regained their composure and bolted after him.

Jack headed for the old church. Racing into the bell tower, key in hand, he climbed the wooden stairs. High above him, dangling from the timbers was the skeleton of the legendary hanged priest. Jack gave the skeleton a quick nod and continued his climb.

Norrington and Will quickly caught up to Jack on the stairs. Norrington started swinging his sword at Jack. But Jack stepped aside just in time. The weapon whistled as it moved past his arm. With a grunt, Norrington slammed Jack with the hilt of his sword, grabbed the key, and flung Jack from the stairway.

As Jack fell, he reached out and grabbed the bell tower rope that held the priest's skeleton. Jack and the skeleton both dropped straight down. But Will grabbed the second rope and was hoisted up just as Jack was making his way down. Will snatched the key from Norrington as he passed him near the top of the tower. When Will reached the top of the tower, the church bell began to toll.

Chapter 30

Down on the beach, a gentle ripple appeared in the water. Slowly and eerily, the heads of Jones's crew rose from the pale blue water, and the fearsome gang stalked ashore. They gathered at the now-empty, recently dug hole.

Suddenly, the sound of the church bells drew the crew's attention to the tower, and they watched as Will Turner stepped out onto the church's rooftop.

Will was trying to get away . . . from Jack, Norrington, and now Jones's crew. He jumped across a break in the roof as Norrington slashed at him over the gaping void. Using the point of his sword, Norrington nimbly lifted the key from Will's grasp. The former commodore felt the sudden weight of the key as it dropped into his hand, then felt it disappear just as quickly as Jack snatched it away from him.

Norrington turned in a rage and knocked Jack's sword from his hand. He looked over his shoulder at Will. "Excuse me while I kill the man who ruined my life," he said, pardoning himself.

"Be my guest," Will answered, finally relaxing for a moment.

Jack raised a finger. "Let's examine that claim for a moment, shall we, former commodore."

Will couldn't help but smile as Jack once again tried to turn the odds in his favor. "Who was the man who, at the moment you had a notorious pirate safely behind bars and a beautiful dolly belle bound for the bridal, saw fit to free said pirate and take your dearly beloved for himself?" Jack nodded toward Will.

Norrington didn't let Jack continue. "Enough!" he roared slashing wildly at Jack. Unarmed, Jack threw up his hands and slid down the roof screaming. The key dropped to the ground.

"Good show!" Will said, clapping.

"Unfortunately, Mr. Turner," Norrington said, turning his blade on Will, "he's right." Norrington hated Jack, but he wasn't fond of Will, either.

Below them, Jack took advantage of the

fight above, grabbing the key and running. "Still rooting for you, mate!" he called up to Will as swords clashed.

Jack slowed to a walk and put the key over his neck. Just when he thought he was safe, he stumbled into an open grave.

As Jack tried to get out of the hole, Will leaped on to a mill wheel that was attached to the side of the church. The old wheel creaked under his weight. Norrington jumped on as well, and, with a huge crash, the wheel suddenly broke free. Will and Norrington steadied their legs to keep balanced.

Just as Jack finally pulled himself out from the grave, he was caught up by the rolling wheel. The key fell away from Jack's neck and was hooked on a splintered nail on the surface of the wheel. A moment later Jack was thrown off the wheel. He had lost the key . . . again! He sighed and then took off after the runaway wheel.

Chapter 31

Meanwhile, in the small island's jungle, Elizabeth had finally caught up with Pintel and Ragetti.

"'Ello, Poppet," Pintel said, grinning, as Elizabeth confronted them. He and Ragetti set down the chest and pulled their swords. Elizabeth reached for hers but suddenly remembered Will had taken it. Slowly, she began to back away.

The two pirates were about to attack when something came crashing through the jungle. The three turned to see the mill wheel roll past with Jack running full speed behind it.

Pintel and Ragetti shrugged, focusing again on Elizabeth. Suddenly, a barnacle-encrusted axe hit a tree next to Ragetti's head with a twang. Jones's crew had arrived.

Pintel and Ragetti dropped their swords at Elizabeth's feet in horror. They grabbed the chest and made a run for it. Elizabeth took a sword in each hand, racing through the trees behind them.

Running as fast as they could, and still holding the chest, the pirates tried to pass on either side of a tree and slammed the chest smack into its trunk. Jones's crew suddenly burst through the jungle. Looking at the trunk, then at the imposing and terrifying crew, Ragetti, Pintel, and Elizabeth made a quick decision: the three of them took off at lightning speed and left the chest behind.

But on another part of the island, a chase was still going on. Jack was after the wheel, which held the key to what was *in* the chest. He picked up some speed and for the first time was running *next* to the wheel instead of *behind* it. Focusing on the key as it looped around, Jack timed his move perfectly and jumped back into the wheel.

From his spot on top, Will saw what Jack was doing. Will reached down, grabbed the key from the nail, and swung himself back inside the wheel. Norrington was quick to follow. Slashing at Will, Jack grabbed the key, climbed on to the top, and then jumped into a nearby palm tree.

Dangling from the palm, Jack noticed one of Jones's crew members coming—and he was carrying the chest! Jack reached for a coconut. Happy with the weight of it, he hurled it at the crewman's head.

Jack saw the undead crewman's head roll off as it was thwacked by his well-placed coconut. He jumped down. No other crewmen were in sight. With the key in hand and almost unable to believe his good fortune, he carefully approached the chest.

Jack took a breath. Kneeling beside the chest, he turned the key in the lock. His eyes widened as he finally saw what he'd been searching for: Jones's heart. Taking off his shirt, he reached into the chest and wrapped the heart safely up. Then he glanced around one more time to make sure he hadn't been spotted, and took off.

Jack dashed directly to the longboat. He reached into the bow and grabbed his jar. Emptying some of the dirt onto the beach, he placed the covered heart inside and filled the jar back up with sand.

Jack looked up when he heard a sudden commotion. Bursting from the jungle came Pintel,

Ragetti, and Elizabeth. They were again hauling the chest, and Jones's crewman were close behind.

Elizabeth bravely slashed away at Jones's crew, but her efforts were increasingly futile. She was about to be overrun, when the huge wheel came crashing from out of the jungle.

The wheel rolled over several of Jones's crewmen, which allowed Elizabeth to catch up to Pintel and Ragetti as they dragged the chest through the sand toward the longboat.

Jack gritted his teeth, unhappy with how crowded the beach had become. He tucked his jar back into the bow and raised an oar ready to shove off or fight.

The huge wheel finally lumbered to the waterline and tilted over with a splash. Will and Norrington dizzily climbed out. Norrington staggered over to the longboat and collapsed over the edge. He lifted his head, and his eyes fell on Jack's jar. He reached into the bow.

Jack held his breath. He watched as Norrington's hand moved past the jar and reached for the Letters of Marque in his coat pocket. Jack didn't try to stop him. He had no need for those papers now, not when he had the heart that controlled Davy Jones and safe passage or peril for every ship that sailed the seven seas.

As Jack contemplated his good fortune, the fight on the beach raged on—it was now Sparrow's crew versus Jones's crew . . . and Jones seemed to have the advantage.

Suddenly, through the chaos, Will noticed the chest. The key was still in the lock. He leaned down to open it, when Jack quickly spun around with an oar in hand and whacked him in the head. Will dropped to the beach . . . unconscious. Rushing to his side, Elizabeth looked down at her fiancé.

"We're not getting out of this," Elizabeth said to Norrington when she realized just how desperate the situation had become.

"Not with the chest," he replied, knowing what had to happen. He quickly grabbed the chest and ordered her into the boat. "Don't wait for me," he called back and disappeared from the beach into the jungle. Jones's crew took off after him.

"I say we respect his final wish," Jack said quickly from his spot nearby.

"Aye!" Pintel agreed and began pushing the longboat into the surf. Jack hopped in and grabbed his jar. He had the heart, but didn't want to take any chances. Holding on to the heart, and Tia Dalma's dirt inside the jar, he'd be safe.

"We have to take Will," Elizabeth ordered. Jack rolled his eyes, but nodded his head, and Pintel and Ragetti hauled Will into the longboat. Without another word, they pushed off . . . leaving Norrington behind.

Chapter 32

$\mathfrak{M}$oments later, Jack's crew, minus Norrington, was back on the main deck of the *Black Pearl*. Will slowly opened his eyes. "What happened to the chest?" he asked groggily.

"Norrington took it—to draw them off," Elizabeth answered.

Gibbs appeared on deck and welcomed them all back. He was ready to make sail. "Jack!" he said. "We spied the *Dutchman* an hour past, rounding the point!"

"Is that so?" Jack replied with a confident look in his eye.

Gibbs gave his captain a funny look. He didn't have time to try and figure out what was going on. There was a dangerous ship—the *most* dangerous ship to ever sail the seas—far too close. "All hands! Set sail! Run her full!" Gibbs shouted.

As the *Pearl*'s crew scrambled to get underway, Jack felt no need to rush. He sat himself down on a barrel, his legs dangling, and cradled his precious jar.

"Gibbs, is your throat tight?" he asked.

"Aye," Gibbs answered.

Jack nodded. "Your heart beats fast, your breath is short, you have an acute awareness of the vulnerability of your own skin?"

"Aye! Aye!"

"I fear you suffer from the malady of intense and overwhelming fear," Jack observed casually.

"What's into you? We've got only half a chance at best—and that's if the wind holds!" Gibbs said, not understanding Jack's attitude. Only a few hours before, Jack had been a bundle of nerves himself.

Elizabeth walked to the rail. For once, she had to agree with Jack. "We are in no danger," she said to Gibbs. "I see empty horizon in all directions."

She had spoken too soon. As they watched in horror, the ocean began to bubble and foam. Suddenly, with a mighty splash, the *Flying Dutchman* shot up from below the sea. It settled down right next to the *Pearl*, sending a wave over her decks.

"Hard to port! Steal his wind! Full canvas!" Gibbs shouted with all his might.

As the crew worked furiously at their stations, Jack turned toward the *Dutchman*. Lifting the jar over his head, he pointed to it, nodded, smiled, and gave a friendly wave.

At the helm of the *Flying Dutchman*, Davy Jones pulled back as if he'd been struck, realizing that Jack must have his heart.

"Ready the cannons," Jones said to Maccus.

Jack yelled out to the *Dutchman*, "Over here! Yoo-hoo! Parlay!"

Gibbs moved alongside. "What's your play, Jack?"

"Shhh!" Jack replied. He thumped the jar. "I have the heart. In here," Jack whispered.

"Bless me! How?" Gibbs asked.

Jack smiled. "I'm Captain Jack Sparrow, remember?"

Gibbs sighed as he watched the cannon ports on the *Dutchman* opening. Jack thought he was invincible, but Gibbs knew better—he had to protect the ship. "Hard a port!" he shouted, turning his attention back to the ship. "Hurry, men!"

Jack's crew scrambled, and the *Black Pearl* tacked hard, leaving the *Dutchman* at her stern.

A blast of cannon fire suddenly came from the *Dutchman's* forward guns. "Into the swells! Go square to the wind! Come on!" Gibbs yelled, adjusting course.

The *Dutchman* fired again, but the *Pearl* was pulling away. "She's falling behind!" Elizabeth cheered.

"Aye! With the wind, we've got her!" Gibbs nodded proudly.

"The *Black Pearl* can outrun the *Dutchman*?" Will asked him.

"That ain't a natural ship," Gibbs said, nodding to the *Flying Dutchman*. "It can sail direct against the wind, into a hurricane and not lose speed. That's how she takes her prey. But with the wind . . ."

"We rob her advantage," Will said, suddenly understanding.

"Aye," Gibbs said. "The *Pearl* is the only ship Davy Jones fears. With reason."

Chapter 33

Jack smiled as the *Pearl* sped farther and farther away from the *Dutchman*. He held his jar close.

"If we can outrun her, we can take her!" Will said rushing to Jack on deck. "We should turn and fight!"

"Or flee like the cowardly weasels we are," Jack answered brightly.

"You've the only ship as can match the *Dutchman*! In a fair fight we've got half a chance."

"That's not much incentive for me to fight fair, is it?" Jack answered, drumming upon his jar.

Suddenly, the *Black Pearl* lurched. Sailors tumbled forward. Jack's jar was knocked free from his hands and shattered, sending sand and dirt all over the deck. He dropped to his knees and pawed through it. There was nothing more than the dirt and sand.

Jack looked up at Gibbs and swallowed hard. "Um. I *don't* have the heart."

"Then who does?" Gibbs asked as the *Pearl* groaned and shuddered to a stop. Jack went pale. He had neither Jones's heart, nor did he have Tia Dalma's dirt.

Elizabeth looked out over the rail as the *Pearl* ground to a halt.

"We must have hit a reef!" she called out.

Will frowned, he'd heard those same words aboard the *Edinburgh Trader*. "No! It's not a reef! Get away from the rail!"

"What is it?" Elizabeth asked, seeing the terror in Will's eyes.

"The Kraken," was all Gibbs said.

Chapter 34

The deck of the *Pearl* grew silent as Gibbs's words sunk in. The Kraken had finally found Jack.

On the floor of the ship, Jack had stopped shifting through the dirt and sand. It was no use. The heart was not there, and the Black Spot had reappeared on his hand. He was marked, the situation was hopeless—he was doomed.

As quietly as possible, Jack headed toward the *Pearl*'s stern. None of the crew members noticed as he slipped into a longboat and rowed away from his ship.

The water around the *Pearl* began to churn and bubble, indicating the arrival of the Kraken. Then, the terrible creature appeared from the depths, tentacles held high above the crew.

"To arms!" Will shouted. "Defend the masts! Don't let it get a grip." The pirates ran to their stations and prepared for the coming attack. Cannons were loaded and masts made ready.

Slowly, the Kraken's tentacles made their way over the railings. But Will had known that the Kraken would attack on the starboard side from his earlier encounter with the creature, and the cannons were ready. With a powerful command from Will, the cannons were fired. The Kraken was blown away—its body twisting in pain as it sank back away from the ship, smashing the longboats as it went down.

"It will be back!" Will yelled. Turning to Elizabeth he added, "Get off the ship."

"No boats," Elizabeth replied. The Kraken had destroyed every last one of them. Or, almost every last one . . .

As the Kraken was getting ready to attack again, Jack was working on getting away in his longboat as quickly as possible. But there was something stopping him from making a clean break. He looked down at his Compass and watched the needle swing to its mark—the *Black Pearl* and his crew.

With a sigh, Jack began to row.

* * *

Back on the *Pearl*, it looked like the Kraken was going to win this battle. Nothing the pirates did to stop the monster worked. They shot at it, stabbed at it, threw nets at it . . . but the beast kept coming.

Elizabeth stood in the captain's cabin, a rifle in her shaking hands. She knew Jack had disappeared and was furious. How could he leave at a time like this? He was the one the Kraken was looking for. He had gotten them into this mess. Then, tentacles slowly moved through the windows and started toward her.

Stumbling, she dropped the rifle, headed toward the deck and ran straight into Jack. He was back.

"We've got some time. Abandon ship!" he ordered, ignoring Elizabeth's look of surprise.

"What chance do we have in a boat?" Will asked, coming over to Jack.

"Very little. But we can make for the island. We can get away as it takes down the *Pearl*!" As Jack said this, his eyes grew sad. There was no choice. The Kraken would return and the *Pearl* would go under. They had to get away.

Following orders, Will, Gibbs, and the rest

of the crew headed toward the longboat. But Elizabeth lingered behind.

"Thank you, Jack," Elizabeth said softly. Moving closer toward him, she added, "You came back. I always knew you were a good man."

Leaning forward, Elizabeth kissed the pirate, then stepped back slowly.

CLICK.

Jack glanced down. Elizabeth had chained him to the mast of the boat while they kissed. "It's after you, not the ship . . . not us. It's the only way," she explained.

"Pirate," Jack said, with admiration.

Elizabeth took one last look at the pirate who had been the cause of so much trouble in her life and the cause of so much adventure. She rushed off the ship and left Jack . . . waiting. Slowly, the tentacles of the Kraken snaked onboard. With a mighty roar, the creature rose up in front of him—its mouth gaping and its breath deadly. And there before Jack, in the teeth of the mighty Kraken, was Jack's lost, beloved hat. He plucked it out of the monster's mouth and placed it back on his head where it belonged.

"Hello, beastie," Jack said.

From the longboat, the crew of the *Black Pearl* watched as the Kraken and Jack battled. Slowly, the entire ship was covered by the terrible creature. With one mighty splash, the ship, and Jack with it, was taken below the waves.

Onboard the *Flying Dutchman*, Davy Jones smiled. "Jack Sparrow," he said with satisfaction, "our debt is settled."

But Jones was not the only soul watching from the *Dutchman*. Bootstrap Bill was looking on, as well. As Jack went down with the ship, Bootstrap's eyes grew wide with shock. What was left of Bootstrap's cursed heart wrenched.

With eyes full of sorrow, Bootstrap Bill looked out toward the still water where Jack and the *Pearl* had so recently been sailing. He remembered Jack Sparrow—*Captain* Jack Sparrow—with a heavy heart. Quietly and painfully, Bill whispered out toward the empty sea, "If any man could beat the devil, I'd have thought it would be you."

The *Black Pearl* was gone, along with her captain. And, already, the world seemed a bit less bright without them.

Beginning Spring 2006, Disney Press presents a series of all-new novels featuring Captain Jack Sparrow's years as a teenage stowaway. Here's a sneak peek at volume one . . .

The Coming Storm

By Rob Kidd

CHAPTER ONE

A dim moon rose over the ocean as the wind blew thickening clouds across the sky. Faint shadows were cast up on the island below: Huge, black sailing ships, sea monsters, and other things that haunted the midnight waters seemed to cascade over the hills. Few stars were strong enough to twinkle through the stormy haze. The white sands of the beach were swept into little whirlwinds, shifting the patterns on the sand dunes.

A bad night for sailing.

The few respectable citizens of Tortuga

stayed snug in their well-guarded houses. Everyone else—buccaneers, swashbucklers and cutthroats all—was down at the Faithful Bride, drinking ale and rum.

Between gusts of wind from the gathering storm, the noise from the tavern could be heard a half mile away. Laughing, shouting, and the occasional burst of gunfire echoed through the night as drinkers took up a shanty they all knew:

Blow high! Blow low! And so sailed we.
I see a wreck to windward and a lofty ship
  to lee,
A-sailing down all on the coasts of High
  Barbary. . . .

From outside, the Faithful Bride looked like nothing more than an oversize shack. It wasn't even built out of proper wood, but from the timbers of wrecked boats. It smelled like a boat, too: tar and salt and sea-weed and fish. When a light rain finally began to fall, the roof leaked in a dozen places.

Inside, no one seemed to care about the puddles on the floor. Tankards were clashed together for toasts, clapped on the table for refills, and occasionally thrown at some-one's head.

It was crowded tonight, every last shoddy chair filled in the candle-lit tavern. *I reckon we have enough old salts here to crew every ship in Port Royal*, the Faithful Bride's young bar-maid, Arabella, thought. She was clearing empty mugs off a table surrounded by men who were all hooting at a story. Like everyone in the pub, they were dressed in the tattered, mismatched garb common to all the "sailors" of the area: ragged breeches, faded waistcoats, stubbly beards, and the odd sash or belt.

One of them tugged on her skirt, grinning toothlessly.

Arabella rolled her eyes and sighed. "Let me guess," she said, tossing aside her tangled auburn locks. "Ale, ale, ale and . . . oh, probably another ale?"

The sailor howled with laughter. "That's my lass!"

Arabella took a deep breath and moved on to the other tables.

"There's no Spanish treasure left but inland, ye daft sprog," a sailor swore.

"I'm not talkin' about *Spanish* treasure," his friend, the second-rate pirate Handsome Todd said, lowering his voice. There was a gleam in his eye, not yet dulled by drink. "I'm talkin' about Aztec Gold, from a whole *lost kingdom*. . . ."

Arabella paused and listened in, pretending to pick a mug up off the floor.

"Yer not talking about Stone-Eyed Sam

and *Isla Esquelética*?" the sailor replied, skeptically. "*Legend* says Sam 'e had the Sword of Cortés, and 'e cursed the whole island. Aye, I agree with only one part of that story—that it's *legend*. Legend, mate. 'A neat little city of stone and marble—just like them there Romans built,' they say. Bah! Rubbish! Aren't nothing like that in the Caribbean, I can tell you!"

"Forget the blasted kingdom and the sword, it's his *gold* I'm talking about," Handsome Todd spat out. "And *I* can tell you, I *know* it's real. Seen it with my own eyes, I have. It changes hands often, like it's got legs all its own. But there are ways of finding it."

"Ye got a ship, then?" the first sailor said with a leery look in his eyes.

"Aye, a fine little boat, perfect for slipping in and out of port unseen . . ." Handsome Todd began. But then he noticed Arabella, who was pretending to wipe something from the floor with her apron. She looked up and gave him a weak smile.

She looked again at the floor and rubbed fiercely with the edge of her apron. "Blasted men, spillin' their ale," she said.

Handsome Todd relaxed. But he looked around suspiciously as if the other buccaneers, the walls, or the King himself were listening. "Let's go somewhere a bit quieter, then, shall we? As they say, *dead men tell no tales.*"

Arabella cursed and moved away. Usually, no one cared—no one *noticed* if she were there or not. To the patrons of the Bride, she was just the girl who filled the tankards. She had heard hundreds of stories and legends over the years. Each story was almost like being on an adventure.

Almost.

Still, she decided, *not a bad night, considering.*

It could have been far worse. A storm often seemed to bring out the worst in an already bad lot of men.

And then, suddenly, the door blew open with gale force.

A crash of lightning illuminated the person in the doorway. It was a stranger, wet to the bone. Shaggy black hair was plastered against his head, and the lightning glinted in his eyes. Arabella held her breath—she had never seen anyone like him before.

Then the door slammed shut, and the candlelight revealed an angry, dripping, young man—no older than Arabella. There was silence for a moment. Then the patrons shrugged and returned to their drinks.

The stranger began to make his way through the crowd, eyes darting left and right, up and down like a crow's. He was obviously looking for someone, or some-*thing*. His jaw was set in anger.

His hazel eyes lit up for a moment: he must have found what he was looking for. He bent down behind a chair, and reached for something. Arabella stood on her tiptoes to see—it just looked like an old sack. Not at all worth stealing from the infamous pirate who was guarding it.

"Oh, no . . ." Arabella whispered.

The stranger bit his lip in concentration. He stretched his fingers as long and narrow as possible, discretely trying to reach between the legs of the chair.

Without warning—and without taking the drink from his lips—the man who sat in the chair rose up, all seven feet and several hundred pounds of him. His eyes were the color of a storm, and they sparked with anger.

The stranger pressed his palms together and gave a quick bow.

"Begging your pardon, Sir, just admiring

my . . . I mean *your* fine satchel there," he said, extremely politely.

The pirate roared and brought his heavy tankard down, aiming for the stranger's head.

The stranger grabbed the sack and side-stepped just in time. The mug whistled past his ear . . .

. . . and hit another pirate behind him.

This other pirate wasn't as big, but he was just as irritable. And armed. *And* he thought the stranger was the one who had just hit him in the head with a tankard! The pirate drew a rapier and lunged for the stranger.

The stranger scooted backward, moving out of the way of the deadly blade. His second attacker kept going, falling forward into the table where the giant pirate had been sitting. The rickety table broke under his weight, and drinks, coins, and knives flew into the air. The buccaneers around the table leapt up, drawing their swords and pistols.

It didn't take much to start a barroom brawl in Tortuga.

The Faithful Bride exploded with the sounds of punches, groans, screams, yells and hollers, the clash of cutlasses striking rapiers, and the snap of wood as chairs were broken over heads. All this, in addition to the sound of the crashing thunder and the leaking ceiling that began to pour down on the brawling patrons.

The stranger was caught in the middle of it. And to make matters worse, the giant pirate was still after him.

The huge pirate drew his sword and swung it at the stranger. The stranger leapt up onto the chair behind him, the blade slicing the air where he had just stood.

"That's a bit close, mate," the stranger said. He jumped off the chair again and kicked at one of its legs, causing it to flip up into the air and land in his hands.

The giant swung again, but the stranger held the chair like a shield, blocking every strike. Bits of wood flew off the chair where the blade hit.

Another pirate dove for the stranger—or maybe for someone behind him, it was hard to tell at this point. The stranger leaned out of the way, just barely avoiding the collision, and his attacker toppled into the giant pirate.

With the giant now otherwise engaged, the stranger hoisted the sack onto his shoulder, turned around and surveyed the scene behind him. What was—for pirates—a fairly quiet night of drinking, had turned into yet another bloody and violent brawl like the others he'd seen in his day. He couldn't resist grinning.

"Huh. Not a *single* bruise on me," he said out loud. "Not one blasted scratch on *Jack Sparrow*."

Then someone smashed a bottle against a timber above his head. The giant had risen behind him, surprisingly quiet for such a large man. Jack swung around to see him and began to back away.

"You'll just be giving me that sack now, boy" the pirate said in a deadly voice, holding the broken bottle before him and pointing it at Jack.

"Uh . . ." Jack looked around, but he was surrounded by the fight on all sides, still blocked from the door.

"Good Sir . . ." he began, hoping something would come to him. But before he could think of a way out of this one, the giant roared and bolted forward.

The adventure continues May 2006.

Available wherever books are sold.